HAUNTED HOUSES

Also available in Piccolo True Adventures

Piccolo True Adventures

HAUNTED HOUSES

AIDAN CHAMBERS

Illustrations by John Cameron Jarvies

A Piccolo Original

PAN BOOKS LTD
LONDON

First published 1971 by Pan Books Ltd,
33 Tothill Street, London, SW1.

ISBN 0 330 02820 0

2nd Printing 1971
3rd Printing 1972
4th Printing 1973

Printed and Bound in England by
Hazell Watson & Viney Ltd,
Aylesbury, Bucks

Contents

From the Author

The stories in this book are about ghosts that have haunted people's houses. All of them are supposed to be true, but sometimes it is difficult to know which ones really are true and which ones are not.

Sid Mularney's experiences in his motorcycle workshop sound pretty persuasive (p. 105). Certainly he believed they were caused by ghosts – and he still does believe it, for he is alive and well and goes on working in Leighton Buzzard where it all happened a few years ago. But I wonder whether Myles Phillipson had quite such a bad time as he gets from Dorothy and Kraster Cook in 'The Ghostly Skulls of Calgarth Hall' (p. 78).

To be honest, I'm not very concerned whether these hauntings are true or not. They make good stories, and that – to me, at least – is the important thing. I have never seen a ghost, though I believe they exist. And I am not a ghost hunter (there are such people); I do not go around hoping to meet ghosts. Nor do I belong to the Society for Psychical Research, whose members try to investigate scientifically ghosts people claim to have seen.

Whether the hauntings in this book ever really happened or not, I hope you will enjoy reading about them. Perhaps you would like to write and tell me what you think of them, and about any experiences you've had with ghosts, or about the ghosts who are supposed to haunt places near where you live. If you do, you should send your letter to me at this address: Pan Books Ltd, 33 Tothill Street, London SW1.

CHAPTER ONE

The Man Who Did Not Believe in Ghosts

Everywhere in Britain there are haunted houses. Many of them are fine old castles or great manors that have been lived in for hundreds of years. You almost expect such places to have a ghost or two tucked away somewhere among the creaking stairways and old dark corridors and dim panelled rooms. But there are other houses, ordinary family homes, neither very old nor very ghostly-looking where people say they have seen ghosts. Or heard them. Or, most frightening of all, *felt* them.

Some ghosts belong to once-famous people; others, most in fact, belong to people whose names have long since been forgotten, and who are remembered now only because their spirits haunt the places where once they lived and, usually, died. Like the Tower of London, that last cheerless home for many prisoners, innocent and guilty. The Tower is still guarded night and day, so it is not surprising that the many hauntings which take place there have been seen by the men who keep watch.

On the night of February 15th, 1915, the sergeant of

the guard, Mr William Ewart Nicholls, saw one of the Tower ghosts and recorded what happened.

'Just after the guard had been changed at about two o'clock,' wrote Mr Nicholls, 'the officer in charge suddenly pointed and said, "What's that woman doing here at this time of night?"

'We all saw her – dressed in brown, with a ruff, moving quickly towards the river until she disappeared into a stone wall nine feet thick. The warders told us it was the ghost of Anne Boleyn, nearly always seen on the eve of a death in the Tower.'

The First World War was being fought at this time. The morning after Mr Nicholls saw the ghost, a spy was shot in the Tower moat.

Anne Boleyn's ghost is one of the most famous of all, in and out of the Tower. Her headless figure has been seen driving furiously in a ghostly coach along Norfolk roads; and she is said to spend part of every Christmastime under a great oak in Hever Castle grounds, near Edenbridge in Kent, where King Henry VIII wooed her.

She was the second of Henry's famous – and mostly doomed – six wives. When he wanted to get rid of her, he accused Anne of being a witch, and, in days when witches were much feared and often put to death, people believed him. The unfortunate woman was unlucky enough to be born with six fingers on one hand, and this added to people's suspicions of her.

Anne was beheaded on a pleasant spring day, May 19th, 1536. She went to her death laughing and making jokes about her slim neck and the skill of the executioner with his razor-sharp sword. Since that time she has been seen many times in the Tower, with her head, as Mr Nicholls saw her, and without.

One night in the nineteenth century an officer of the guard saw a light in the chapel of St Peter ad Vincular, the chapel where Anne was buried, within the Tower. The officer asked a sentry what was going on in the building. The sentry replied that he did not know, nor did he care to find out. Queer things went on inside that chapel, he said. The officer determined to find out for himself. He sent the sentry for a ladder, which he leaned against one of the chapel windows. Then he climbed up, and peered into the building.

He saw, by an eerie light that filled the inside of the chapel, a procession of people dressed in Elizabethan clothes walking up the aisle. At the head of the procession was a woman whose face, the officer said later, was like the famous painting of Anne Boleyn. He watched spellbound while the ghostly crowd walked up the chapel, and then suddenly vanished as did the eerie light, leaving the chapel empty and in darkness again.

In 1864 a sentry was court-martialled for being found asleep on watch. He defended himself by claiming that he had really been lying in a faint after seeing Anne Boleyn's ghost.

The court would not believe the soldier's story, but he stuck to it. He had been on duty by the Lieutenant's Lodging, he said, when suddenly he saw a white figure coming towards him. He challenged it, but it kept on approaching, so he thrust his bayonet into it. Instantly there was a fiery flash which ran up his rifle and gave him such a shock that he dropped his weapon and fainted. He described what he had seen as 'the figure of a woman wearing a queer-looking bonnet, but there was no head inside'.

Still the court refused to believe the soldier. So he called several witnesses, other soldiers. Each one testified that he had seen a headless woman near the Lieutenant's Lodging that night.

The turning point in the trial came when an officer gave evidence that he had been in his room in the Bloody Tower when he heard the sentry make the challenge, 'Who goes there?' The officer had looked out of the window and had seen the sentry with the white figure walking towards him. He watched as the sentry thrust his bayonet at the ghost, but, the officer stated, the spectre had walked through the bayonet and the sentry, who had then collapsed to the ground. A few minutes later he was found unconscious, and accused of sleeping on watch.

The court did not make up its mind whether or not

it really believed that the sentry had seen the ghost of Anne Boleyn, but it judged the soldier Not Guilty of sleeping at his post!

In 1933 a similar thing occurred, though this time the soldier was not arrested. He was on guard duty when he saw the headless woman. Like the sentry those many years before, he thrust at the ghost with his bayonet. But still the figure came onwards. The soldier fled, calling for help as he ran.

Seeing is believing, they say, and most people probably have to see a ghost before they will believe ghosts exist. But some people refuse to believe ghosts *might* exist. It is just not possible, they say, and what people think are ghosts could always be explained away very simply if all the facts were known. Some people have said this – and then changed their minds. Like the man who went to Creslow Manor in Buckinghamshire.

Creslow Manor has a family ghost, the restless spirit of an old lady who died many years ago. She haunts a bedroom in the oldest part of the house, where she has often been heard by people with courage enough to sleep in the room, or to go into it after midnight.

The ghost comes from the cellars, up a staircase that reaches the landing near one of the two doors opening into the bedroom. Inside the room she walks about, sometimes in a slow, grand manner, her long silk dress swishing on the floor; sometimes with noisy violence as though she were locked in a struggle.

'The sentry thrust his bayonet at the ghost'

Few people have dared stay the night in that room more than once; and there are many stories about the fate of those who tried sleeping there. One particular man who visited Creslow and changed his mind about ghosts, came as a guest to a dinner party. During the evening, rain began to fall and by the time the visitor was ready to leave for home the night was pitch black and very wet. His host pressed the visitor to stay at Creslow until morning – provided that he did not object to sleeping in the haunted room, the only room not occupied.

The visitor laughed. 'Object,' he jeered. 'Of course I don't object. I don't believe in all these fanciful stories about ghosts and haunted rooms. I'll sleep there tonight for no other reason than to prove such stories are nonsense.'

The room was got ready. The host asked his guest if he would care to have a fire in his room. The guest refused.

'Then a night light, perhaps?'

'Certainly not.'

Nevertheless, the host ordered that a candle and a box of matches be laid on a table at the bedside in case his guest should need them.

It was nearly midnight when the visitor said good-night and prepared to go up to bed. As a joke, he took down from the wall above the fireplace a brace of pistols and a cutlass, and pretended to arm himself against the horrors to come. Then, with great play-acted seriousness, he said farewell to his host and hostess as though he expected never to see them again. And with that, he went laughing up the stairs.

Next morning dawned bright and fresh after the rain. The family and their guests met for breakfast, cheerful at the prospect of such a lovely day. The meal was almost finished before anyone noticed the absence of the disbelieving visitor.

A servant was sent to his room. He returned to report that he had knocked loudly at the door, but had received no answer.

Two or three of the men at once accompanied the host upstairs. They knocked loudly at the visitor's door, but got no reply. Fearing that something dreadful might have happened, they tried the lock, found the door open and pushed their way inside.

The room was empty. The bed was disturbed, but there was no sign of the missing guest.

The servants were called and asked if any of them had seen the man. No one had. Someone was sent off to the stable to see whether his horse was still there – perhaps he had gone off early on business. But the horse was secure in its stall.

The host and his guests returned puzzled to the breakfast table. And just at that moment the visitor entered the room. He was white-faced and haggard.

He sat down at the table, refreshed himself with tea and food, and told his story.

The night before, he said, he went to his room cheerfully enough and not at all bothered by the tales he had heard of its being haunted. But, to be sure no tricks could be played on him, he carefully locked both the doors that led into the bedroom. He then searched the entire place, found nothing amiss, and noted that there was no way in except by the two locked doors. Well satisfied, he undressed, climbed into bed, and quickly fell asleep.

Some time later, he suddenly found himself wide awake. He did not know what had woken him. The room was pitch black with not a glimmer of light by which to look at his watch. He could not tell how long he had slept.

He was about to turn over and settle himself again, when he heard a strange sound. Raising himself on an elbow, he listened intently. He could hear, unmistakably now, a woman's light-footed tread. The soft steps moved slowly and grandly round the room, followed by the whispering rustle of a long, trailing silk gown.

Determined to find the cause of the noise, the visitor sprang from the bed, groped for the matches, and lit the candle his host had wisely left ready. But there was nothing to be seen, nor now to be heard.

The visitor set about searching the room once more.

He looked under the bed, into the fireplace, up the wide chimney, inside cupboards, and he checked the locks on doors and windows. Everything was as it had been before.

When he checked his watch he saw to his astonishment that the time was only a few minutes after one o'clock. As everything was quiet again, he put out the candle, got back into bed, and soon fell into a deep sleep.

Not for long. This time he was woken by a much louder noise than the first. It was, he said, like the violent movements of someone struggling: the silken dress rustled, the tread was heavy and erratic, and the sounds came abruptly from different parts of the room.

Again the visitor sprang out of bed. But rather than light the candle, he ran to the spot where the noise seemed to come from and tried to grasp the intruder in his arms. His arms met together, empty.

The noise, however, came at once from elsewhere in the room. The visitor followed it, groping with his hands near the floor so that nothing could escape by slipping underneath his grasp.

Round and round the room the now terrified man pursued the violent noise. Each time he reached the spot where the noise came from it moved to another place. As he chased the sounds in the unlit room, he stumbled against furniture, stubbing his bare feet, barking the skin off his hands against the walls. And all to no avail. He caught nothing, saw nothing. But heard all the while, first here then there, the silken rustle and the hurried, struggling steps.

At last the noise ceased as suddenly as it had begun just by the door which opened on to the stairs that led to the cellar. The room was again as quiet as the grave.

The shaken guest lit the candle and set the room to rights, replacing the furniture he had scattered in his frantic chase after the fearful noise. When he had calmed himself, he climbed into bed. But he could not sleep, nor could he bring himself to blow out the light. He lay propped up in bed, all the while expecting the strange sounds to begin again. They never did.

With relief the guest watched the dawn light slowly dispel the darkness of the night. When the sun rose, he got up, weary and tired, and, so that he could escape from that dreadful room, he quietly left the house and spent the time until breakfast walking in the freshness of the morning air.

Who is the ghost of Creslow Manor? Why does she come from the cellar and struggle round that upstairs room? No one knows. The only certain thing is that the visitor left the house on that bright, rain-washed day far less sure that ghosts do not exist than when he had arrived as a dinner guest the night before.

CHAPTER TWO

The Ghost of Owd Nance – and Her Skull

Burton Agnes Hall is a large and beautiful Jacobean house in the East Riding of Yorkshire. It stands close to a small village, between Bridlington and Driffield.

The house was built by three sisters. They never married and when their father died he left them great wealth. One of the sisters, Anne, felt they should build a house that suited their riches and importance. She engaged the best architects, craftsmen and artists, and watched over their work right down to the smallest detail. Anne, called Owd Nance by those who lived in the area, watches over the house still. It is her ghost and skull that haunt the place.

It happened that when the house was finished, much to the sisters' pride and satisfaction, Anne went one day to visit the St Quintin family who lived not far away at Harpham. She went alone, walking the mile or so to her friends' house accompanied only by her dog.

At nightfall, Anne set off for home. As she neared a place called St John's Well, she saw two rough-looking tramps lying on the grass by the side of the well. She approached the men feeling a little afraid, for many tramps in those days made a living by robbing defence-less people in lonely places. But Anne had her dog as protection so she felt there was no real cause for worry, and she pressed on.

When she reached the well the tramps stood up and politely begged for money. Thinking it best to humour them, Anne took out her purse and gave the tramps a few coins. But as she did so the light of the setting sun glinted on a ring she wore. The tramps saw it and demanded rudely that she hand it over at once.

Anne refused. The ring, she said, was not valuable, but it was precious to her because it was an heirloom inherited from her dead mother.

'Mother or no mother,' said one of the tramps harshly, 'we mean to have it. Give it freely, or we'll take it by force.'

Without waiting for answer, he grabbed hold of Anne's hand and tried to pull the ring from her finger.

There was a scuffle. The dog barked and tried to bite the attackers. But while one of them held on to Anne, the second drove the animal away with brutal blows from a stick he carried.

Anne screamed loudly and shouted for help.

'Stop that noise!' cried the second man, and he raised his stick in the air and hit Anne heavily on the head. She fell unconscious to the ground.

But her screams had not gone unheard. Some villagers came running into sight, and the tramps gave up their efforts to pull the ring from Anne's finger, and scrambled away into the trees.

The villagers found Anne still unconscious, her head bleeding freely through a gaping wound. Lifting her as carefully as they could manage, they carried her limp body back to Harpham Hall. There she was nursed back to her senses, and the next day, although weak and battered, she had recovered enough to be taken to her beloved home. She was put at once to bed.

For many days Anne lay in pain, her strength slowly weakening despite the loving attention of her two sisters and all that the best doctors in Yorkshire could do. During the long days of her sickness, she spoke often of one thing: the pride of her life, the magnificent house she had had such a hand in building.

Finally, with little breath left in her frail body, she called her sisters to her bedside.

'Sisters,' she said, 'never shall I sleep peacefully in my grave unless I, or part of me at least, remain here in our beautiful home as long as it lasts. Promise me, dear sisters, that when I am dead my head shall be taken from my body and preserved within these walls. Here let it remain for ever, and on no account be removed. And understand, and make known to those who in future shall become the possessors of the house, that if they disobey this my last request, my spirit shall make such a disturbance within its walls as to render it uninhabitable for others as long as my head is kept from its home.'

The sisters were horrified by Anne's request. But she would hear no arguments, and so to calm her and set her fevered mind at rest, the sisters agreed to do as she asked, though, of course, they dismissed the idea from their minds at once. Anne was ill, they thought, and did not know what she was saying. Soon

'*Her body was buried in the churchyard nearby*'

afterwards she   died. Her body was buried in the churchyard nearby.

The sisters missed Anne bitterly. She had been the most cheerful of the three women, the most talkative, the most active. Now she was gone and their life was dull; in the days that followed Anne's funeral, her sisters dearly wished her back with them.

A week to the day after Anne's death, late in the evening, the two surviving sisters were on the point of going to bed when suddenly they heard a loud crash in one of the upstairs rooms. They rushed to the foot of the stairs and listened and were joined a few minutes later by the servants, also startled by the loud and violent noise.

The sisters ordered two of the menservants to go up and see what had caused the din. The men climbed the stairs and searched the upper rooms. They returned having found nothing unusual or out of place.

Everyone grew very frightened. For a long time they stayed together in a nervous group, not one of them able to pluck up courage and go to bed. At length, however, having heard nothing more, they went to their rooms.

A few days passed without further cause for alarm. But again, exactly a week later, in the dead of night the household was woken by what sounded like many doors being slammed shut in every part of the building.

Sisters and servants ran from their rooms, candles in hand, and met on the landing. Their shadows flickered on the walls about them, their faces were white, and dressed in their nightgowns with their hair disarranged from sleeping, they looked themselves like a gathering of risen ghosts.

Keeping together for comfort and support, they searched the entire house. Every door was fast shut. Yet as they crept from one door to the next, the same terrifying crashes echoed round them, always coming from a part of the house other than where they stood.

When they felt they could bear the resounding noise no longer it ceased as suddenly as it had begun.

Exhausted, shaking with fear, they stopped in their tracks. For what seemed endless seconds the silent group listened breathlessly.

Then one of the servants whispered, 'It seems finished.'

'Do you think,' murmured one of the trembling sisters, 'that it is finished now entirely?'

'Last time, once it had ceased it did not start up again,' said the other.

Cold now so that they no longer knew whether they shivered from fear or from the chill night air, they listened a while longer. The house stood silent, disturbed only by the whisper of their own quick breaths and the cry of an owl outside.

And so at last they returned to their beds. But each

one lay sleepless until daylight banished the fears of the night.

Another quiet week went by. But again, on the same night as twice before, the household had its sleep shattered, this time by the clatter of many people running along the passages and up and down the stairs. The house shook and thundered with the noise until it stopped all at once, only to be followed by something worse. A spine-chilling death-groan that echoed hollowly through the Hall. After the groan, the clattering feet stormed round the house with renewed vigour. Until again the awful groan. And again the stamping feet. And again the groan. On and on through the midnight hours.

No living person left his room that night. No puzzled group met on the landing, no search was made. The inhabitants of Burton Agnes Hall lay in sweats of agonized terror, clutching the bedclothes about their heads.

Next day the women servants gathered their belongings. They could no longer bear the unearthly sounds that broke their sleep each week, they said, and would not remain another night in a house haunted by such an uneasy ghost.

The sisters tried to calm the women. The noises must have a simple explanation, they said; they had nothing to do with ghosts.

Of course they were caused by a ghost, replied the

servants. What else could it be? What simple explanation had been found? None!

And with that they left the Hall.

The sisters, now without help in running their beautiful but very large home, asked the vicar of the parish to visit them. They told him all that had gone on during the three weeks past, and discussed with him every possible solution to the mystery.

During the course of the conversation the sisters remembered, for the first time since Anne had died, the promise they had made to her on her death bed. And they realized then that the noises had been heard on the very same night of the week on which Anne had died. Could it be that their dead sister was keeping now the promise she had made with her dying breath? Her promise to make the house 'uninhabitable for others' if her head was not kept in the home she loved. Surely not! It was unthinkable.

The vicar and the two sisters talked for many hours, trying to find a way of satisfying Anne's wish. In desperation, the vicar finally suggested that Anne's grave should be opened and her coffin looked into in the hope that this might shed some light on the problem. Reluctantly, the sisters agreed.

The following day the vicar and his gravedigger opened Anne's grave. When they reached the coffin and raised the lid a ghastly sight struck horror into both men's hearts. Anne's *body* was as it had been three weeks before when the vicar had last seen it, prepared in its funeral robes. What caused such horror and amazement was Anne's *head*. It was severed from the body and, worse still, the flesh and skin had shrivelled away, leaving a naked skull.

This was enough for the vicar and the sisters. Grotesque and hideous though her wishes seemed, the dead woman had her way: Anne's skull was brought into the Hall.

So it was Owd Nance came home, and while her skull was left in peace the house remained free from ghostly interference. From time to time inhabitants have tried to get rid of the skull. But always the knockings, the resounding footsteps, and the blood-curdling groans have returned to plague the place until it is brought back inside.

Many legends surround the skull by now. One day, it is said, a maid threw it from an upper window onto a passing cart loaded with manure. From the moment the skull landed in the cart the horses were unable to move another step. The waggoner whipped them, but in vain. And it was not until the maid confessed what she had done, and the skull was recovered and brought back into the house, that the horses could manage to pull the cart once more.

A man called Mr Ross, many years ago, wrote an account of one of Owd Nance's hauntings at a time when her skull had been put outside.

Some forty years ago, wrote Mr Ross, John Bilton, a cousin of mine, came from London on a visit to the neighbourhood of Burton Agnes Hall, and having a relative, Matthew Potter, who was game-keeper on the estate and resided at the Hall, he paid him a visit, and was invited to pass the night there. Potter, however, told John that, according to popular report, the house was haunted, and that if he were afraid of ghosts he had better sleep else-where. But John, who was a dare-devil sort of fellow, replied,

'Afraid! Not I indeed. I care not how many ghosts there may be in the house so long as they do not molest me.'

Potter then told him of the skull and of the painted portrait of Owd Nance that hung in one of the rooms, and asked him if he would like to see the picture. John replied that he would, and they went into the room where it was hanging. Potter held a light before the portrait, when, in a moment and without apparent cause, the light went out and defied all attempts to rekindle it. Matthew and John were obliged to grope their way to their bedroom in the dark.

They had to sleep in the same bed, and Matthew was soon asleep and snoring. But John, thinking of the tale of the skull and the curious circumstances of the sudden extinguishing of the light in front of the picture, lay awake. He had been thinking about an hour, when he heard a shuffling of feet outside the bedroom door, which at first he ascribed to the servants going up to bed. But as the sounds did not cease, but kept increasing, he nudged Matthew and said,

'Matty, what the devil is all that row about?'

'Jinny Yewlats [owls],' replied Potter in a half-waking tone, and turning over, again began to snore.

The noises became more frantic, and it seemed ten or a dozen persons were scuffling about in the passage just outside, and rushing in and out of rooms, slamming doors with great violence, upon which John gave his friend another vigorous nudge in the ribs, exclaiming,

'Wake up, Matty. Don't you hear that confounded row? What does it all mean?'

'Jinny Yewlats,' again muttered his companion.

'Jinny Yewlats!' replied John Bilton. 'Jinny Yewlats can't make such an infernal uproar as that!'

Matty, who was now more awake, listened a moment, and then said, 'It's Owd Nance, but I never take any notice of her.' And he rolled over again and began to snore.

After this the fun began fast and furious! A struggling fight seemed to be going on outside, and the clapping of doors reverberated in the passage like thunderclaps. John expected every moment to see the door fly open and Owd Nance with a troop of ghosts come rushing in. But no such a catastrophe occurred, and after a while the noises ceased, and about daybreak John fell asleep.

Mr Ross heard this story from his cousin John the day after the eventful night. John, though he feared little and did not believe in ghosts, told Mr Ross that he had never passed such a frightening night before in his life, and that he would not sleep there again, even if he were offered the Hall itself for doing so.

What about Owd Nance now? Does she still cause the people of Burton Agnes the sleepless nights she has given so many others in her time? Only, it's said, if anyone tampers with her skull, and tries to move it from the house she loved so much. And who can blame her? Burton Agnes Hall remains one of the finest houses in Yorkshire. And the story of Owd Nance is one of the most amazing of all British ghost stories.

CHAPTER THREE

The Artist Who Drew a Ghost

Most people are afraid of ghosts. And, after all, this is not difficult to understand. Anything that can appear and disappear into thin air, can be seen but cannot be touched, can walk through walls and make strange and alarming noises and take on all kinds of shapes is frightening enough. But sometimes someone meets a ghost and feels not at all afraid or shocked. Such a person was Reginald Easton. His ghostly adventures took place about 100 years ago.

Mr Easton earned his living as an artist, and in the course of his work he met the ghost of Thurstaston Old Hall, Cheshire. Afterwards he told the tale to his friend Lord Halifax, who was very interested in ghosts and collected stories about them, which he eventually published in a book called *Lord Halifax's Ghost Book*.

Till his dying day Reginald Easton claimed that his story was true, and here it is. He was invited to visit the Old Hall and paint portraits of the owner's two daughters. When he arrived he found the owner, Mr Cobb, and his wife charming people, and their two daughters very beautiful.

The house was full of guests, so full that Mrs Cobb realized there was only one spare bedroom. For some reason, this embarrassed her; she took her husband to one side and they began talking quietly together. Eventually, Mr Easton heard the words, 'It cannot be helped; there is no other room.' He wondered what was the matter. Was the room damp or draughty or in some other way unpleasant? In an effort to relieve his hostess of worry, he said to Mrs Cobb that he was not at all troubled by dampness or draughts, if this was what bothered her.

'No, no,' said Mr Cobb. 'That is not the problem.' But he would say no more.

That night, Mr Easton had hardly fallen asleep before he woke, sure there was someone in his room. When he opened his eyes he saw, by the light of the moon streaming in through the window, an elderly woman. She was standing at the foot of the bed, her head bent as though she was searching for something on the floor, and rubbing her hands together nervously.

Mr Easton sat up in bed. Thinking that the woman was one of the other guests who had lost her way, he said, 'I beg your pardon, madam, but have you mistaken your room?'

The woman did not reply. Instead, to Mr Easton's astonishment, the figure vanished.

Next morning, during breakfast, the artist was

asked if he had slept well. He answered by relating his strange encounter with the old woman.

'Yes,' said Mr Cobb, 'we never use that room if we can avoid doing so, for our friends are sometimes terrified by the apparition of a dreadful woman who committed a murder in that room.'

It seems that the old woman, many years ago, had lived in the house and wanted it for herself. The only person in her way was a child who had inherited the place from his parents, both of whom had died. One day, the old woman sent the child's nurse away on a false errand. While the nurse was gone, she strangled the poor child, but so skilfully that no one suspected what she had done. So the house became hers.

'Nothing would ever have been known,' said Mrs Cobb, 'if she had not confessed on her deathbed. The property was then sold and Mr Cobb's grandfather bought it.'

Mr Easton wanted to know if the ghost would appear again.

'Certainly she will, and at about the same time,' he was told.

That night the artist prepared himself. On a table at the side of the bed he placed a lamp, turned down as low as possible so that it gave just enough light to see by. At his side on the bed he put a sketch pad and pencil. He determined to stay awake until the ghost

'I am an artist. Will you allow me to make
a sketch of you?'

showed itself, and then to draw the old woman's picture.

Sure enough, the ghostly figure appeared just as it had the night before.

Mr Easton sat up and said, 'I beg your pardon, madam; I am an artist. Will you allow me to make a sketch of you? I shall then convince the sceptics of the truth of . . .'

He got no further. The ghostly woman vanished.

Not to be put off, Mr Easton slept in the room for five nights more. Each night he waited. Each night the ghost appeared, stayed a while, then vanished as mysteriously as it had come. Being an artist, Mr Easton had keen powers of observation and was well trained to remember the details of people's faces, the shape and look of things. He saw enough during his wakeful nights to be able to make a picture of the spectre. That picture he gave to Lord Halifax, who copied it, and placed the copy in his 'Ghost Book'.

Reginald Easton is not the only one to have wanted to get a picture of a ghost. Many others have tried to photograph them. And some have succeeded. Succeeded, that is, if you can believe that the curious shapes of light and shade in their pictures are truly ghosts and not merely tricks of light and reflections caught by the camera!

CHAPTER FOUR

The Haunting of Epworth Parsonage

John Wesley is famous as the founder of the Methodist Church. He was the son of a Church of England minister, Samuel Wesley, who lived for many years at Epworth Parsonage in Lincolnshire. John was born there in 1703.

Between December 1716 and January 1717 some strange events took place at Epworth. Samuel Wesley thought them so unusual that he kept a diary of all that happened. And later his famous son used the diary to write an article about what has now become one of the best-known hauntings in the world.

The Wesley family was devout and intelligent, not very likely to be taken in by things that go bump in the night. Nor would they have made up just for fun, and then had printed as a true account, the story that John and his father had to tell. Everything in the following pages is taken from John Wesley's own article.

The dining-room at Epworth was on the ground floor. One door entered it from the hall, another led straight out into the garden. A little before ten o'clock on the night of December 2nd, 1716, Robert Brown,

Samuel Wesley's manservant, was sitting in the dining-room with a maid when both of them heard knockings on the garden door. Robert got up and looked outside. There was no one there.

Robert closed the door and sat down; but very soon afterwards the two servants heard the knocking again, this time accompanied by a groan.

Two, three times more came the knocking. Each time when Robert opened the door and peered into the night there was no one in sight.

By now the two servants were feeling uneasy, but as there was nothing they could do about the mysterious sounds, they decided to go off to bed.

Robert slept in an attic room at the top of the house. On the attic landing there stood a handmill used for grinding corn. To Robert's surprise, as he reached the landing he saw that the handmill was turning swiftly, all by itself. He must have been a level-headed fellow, for the only thing that vexed him, he said later, was that the mill was empty – otherwise the ghostly power that turned the mill might have done his work for him!

Robert walked past the whirling machine and went to his room. But even there he was not left in peace that night. He had no sooner blown out the candle and climbed into bed than he heard a gobbling noise like a turkey-cock coming from his bedside. This was followed by thumps on the floor as though someone had fallen over boots and shoes left lying about. But Robert knew this was impossible, for even if there was someone in the room besides himself, he had left his boots downstairs and he possessed no shoes at all!

Next day, Robert and the maid told another servant what had gone on the night before.

'What a couple of fools you are!' she said, and laughed heartily. 'I defy anything to frighten me!'

She lived to regret her words. On the evening of the same day she was churning butter. She finished her task, piled the pats of butter on to a tray, and carried them into the dairy. As she entered the room she heard a knocking on a shelf where several bowls of milk were standing. First the rap came from the top of the shelf, then from below.

The maid took a candle and searched above and below the shelf. She found nothing. She was then so frightened that she dropped the tray, butter and all, to the floor and ran from the room as fast as she could.

Nothing more happened until next day between five and six o'clock. John Wesley had a number of sisters. One of them, Molly, then aged about twenty, was sitting in the dining-room reading a book. She heard the door open and someone enter, someone who seemed to be wearing a silk nightdress, for Molly could hear its soft rustle. Wondering, no doubt, who could be dressed for bed at such an early hour, Molly looked up. The door was shut and there was no one else in the room. But the footsteps were audible enough. They walked right round Molly's chair, returned to the door, and then walked round her again.

'It is useless,' Molly thought, 'to run away, for whatever it is that walks round me can certainly run faster than I.'

It must have taken a great deal of self-control to do what Molly did then. She stood up, tucked her book under her arm, and slowly and calmly left the room.

After supper, Molly sat in her bedroom and told her sister Sukey, who was a year older, about her experience with the strange, unearthly footsteps. She related how they had come into the room and walked round her, and how she had heard the rustling of a silk nightgown trailing along behind.

Sukey was haughty. 'I wonder you are so easily frightened,' she said. 'I would like to see anything frighten me!'

There was a table in the centre of the room. Very shortly after Sukey had dismissed Molly's story so lightly, a knocking began underneath the table top. Sukey took the candle, bent down and looked. There was nothing to explain the noise. Just then, the iron casement of the window started to rattle. And the door-latch clacked up and down violently and did not stop for a long time. Sukey forgot all about the boast she had made only a few minutes before. She leapt fully dressed into the bed, pulled the clothes over her head, and would not move from her hiding place until morning.

It was Hetty's turn next. She was nineteen, and another of the Wesley sisters. It was her nightly duty to wait outside her father's room until he had got into bed, and then to take the candle from the room. A few nights after Sukey's fright, Hetty was standing waiting in the corridor as usual, when she heard footsteps coming down the attic stairs. But when they reached the landing no one appeared. On the footsteps came, on towards Hetty, slowly past her, down the main staircase. Every tread seemed to shake the house to the foundations. Hetty stood staring at the empty air, aghast. She could hear the heavy steps as they made their way across the ground floor of the house, up the servants' stairs, and back into the attic.

It was to the eldest Wesley sister, Emilia, that Hetty told her story. Now Emilia had already heard curious noises herself. She described them in a letter written to her brother John when he was writing his article years later.

'My sisters,' she wrote, 'heard noises and told me of them, but I did not much believe till one night, about a week after the first groans were heard. Just after the clock struck ten, I went downstairs to lock the doors, which I always do. Scarce had I got up the west stairs, when I heard a noise like a person throwing down a vast coal in the middle of the kitchen. I was not much frightened but went to my sister Sukey, and we together went all over the lower rooms, and there was nothing out of order. Our dog was fast asleep, and our only cat in the other end of the house. No sooner was I got upstairs and undressing for bed, but I heard a noise . . . This made me hasten to bed.'

When Emilia heard Hetty's story, she tried to put her sister's mind at rest.

'You know I believe none of these things,' she said, and went on, 'Pray let me take away the candle to-night, and I will find out the trick.'

So that night it was Emilia who waited dutifully outside Samuel Wesley's bedroom door. She had just taken the candle from the room when she heard a loud banging in the hall below. She rushed down the stairs, but when she reached the hall, the banging was in the kitchen. She was searching the kitchen for the cause of the row when she heard a knock on the back kitchen door. Softly, she went to the door, turned back the lock and waited. The knock came again. Immediately Emilia pulled the door wide open. There was no one outside.

Emilia closed the door, only to hear the knock again. This time, as she tried to close the door, having again found no one on the other side, it was pushed violently back against her. Emilia struggled, putting her shoulder against the door, and pushed against it as hard as she could. She managed finally to close it, and to turn the key in the lock. Even as she did so the knocking started again. But this time Emilia let it go on and went off to her room.

This was enough: Emilia was finally convinced that no one was playing tricks. She went to her mother and told her all about the strange happenings. Mrs Wesley, like everyone before her, was sceptical.

'If I hear anything myself, I shall know how to judge,' she said.

It was not long before an opportunity presented itself. One day Emilia hurried to Mrs Wesley and begged her to come to the nursery. As the mother and daughter approached the room, they could hear what sounded like a cradle being rocked furiously on the bare wooden floor. But there was no cradle in the room, and there had not been one for many years.

After this Mrs Wesley began to think that perhaps something extraordinary was indeed happening in the house. She consulted her husband.

Samuel Wesley was a very strict father. He had brought up his many children to respect his authority, and he stood for no nonsense. He had heard the children talking among themselves about the strange noises, and he clearly thought it all fanciful rubbish. When his wife came to him with a story of a rocking cradle that nobody could see, he was angry.

'I'm ashamed of you,' he said to Mrs Wesley. 'These boys and girls frighten one another; but you are a woman of sense and should know better. Let me hear of it no more.'

No more did he hear of it – until six o'clock that evening. Every day at six the family met for prayers. One of the prayers was always for the King, and Mr Wesley had just begun this particular prayer when the most thunderous knocking set up from above. And when the prayer had ended and the astonished family had murmured the Amen, the thundering increased to a resounding din. From then on, with very few exceptions, the knockings accompanied morning and evening prayers for as long as the haunting lasted.

After this Mr Wesley himself was worried. He sent his servant, Robert Brown, to the vicar of Haxey, Mr Hoole, asking him to call at the Parsonage. When Mr Hoole arrived, Samuel told him everything he knew about the strange noises and asked his friend's advice. There were by now unaccountable noises in practically every part of the house, and all the family had come across at least one of them. The children had even given a name to the unknown cause of the trouble: 'Old Jeffrey'.

As the two ministers talked together, a servant came into the room and said, 'Old Jeffrey is coming, for I hear the signal.'

This 'signal' was a creaking sound heard every night at quarter to ten coming from the top of the house at the north-east corner. Some people said it was like the sound of a saw cutting wood; others that it resembled a windmill turning stiffly; others that it was like a plane squeaking across a plank.

The servant finished speaking, and from above came a knock.

'Come, sir,' said Mr Wesley to his friend, 'now you shall hear for yourself.'

Upstairs they went, Mr Hoole feeling a little afraid. Mr Wesley took him into the nursery; but the knocks were coming from the room next door. When they went there, however, the knocks were in the nursery. So back they hurried.

They stood in the nursery and listened. The knocking sounded. It was coming from the wooden head of the bed in which Hetty and two of her younger sisters were sleeping. Hetty was trembling and sweating as though in pain or suffering a nightmare.

The sight drove Mr Wesley into a rage. He pulled a pistol from his belt and, to Mr Hoole's surprise and alarm, threatened to shoot at the place on the headboard from which the knocking came. In the nick of time Mr Hoole grabbed Wesley's arm and prevented his pulling the trigger.

'Sir,' he cried, 'you are convinced that this is something supernatural. If so, you cannot hurt it, but you can give it power to hurt you.'

Shaking with anger, Mr Wesley strode over to the bed, bent close to the headboard and said sternly,

'He pulled a pistol from his clothes . . .'

'Thou deaf and dumb devil! Why dost thou fright these children who cannot answer for themselves! Come to me, in my study, that am a man!'

Instantly the knocking ceased.

Samuel Wesley had thrown down a challenge to the spirit that was haunting his house, and the spirit took up the challenge with a vengeance. The worst days of the ghostly activity began.

No one could get into Mr Wesley's study without his knowing, for he kept the only key and the room was always locked if he was not in it. One evening after the issue of the challenge, he went to the study and tried to open the door. It was thrust back into his face with such force that he staggered away, almost thrown to the floor. Recovering, he pushed hard and managed to get the door open and force his way inside.

Presently the knocking began, first on one wall of the room, then on another, and finally from the room next door, which belonged to his daughter Nancy.

Mr Wesley followed the noise there. Nancy was in the room at the time, and she and her father listened to the bangings.

'Speak,' shouted Mr Wesley loudly.

There was no reply, nor did the noise stop.

'These spirits love darkness,' said Mr Wesley to his daughter. 'Put out the candle, and then perhaps it will speak.'

Nancy was fifteen. Like most of the family she was

by now quite accustomed to the noises and would jokingly say she wished that, instead of knocking, the spirit would do her housework for her. The younger children, when they heard the raps on their bedhead, used to say to each other, 'Jeffrey is coming; it is time to go to sleep.' And if they heard a noise during the day, they'd tell their younger sister, 'Hark, Kezzie, Jeffrey is knocking above.' Kezzie would run from room to room chasing the sound, and laughing, and saying what fun she was having.

It was a little nervously that Nancy put out the candle, however: she feared that when she had done so, the spirit would speak and she did not much look forward to that.

Mr Wesley repeated his command in the darkness. But still he got no reply.

'Nancy,' he said, 'two Christians are too much of a match for the devil. Go downstairs. It may be when I am alone he will have the courage to speak.'

Gladly, Nancy left her father to confront the ghost alone.

Mr Wesley was the father of nineteen children, some of whom had died while very small. One of these was a son named after him. Now Mr Wesley called out, 'If thou art the spirit of my son Samuel, I pray thee knock three knocks, no more.'

Immediately the knocking stopped and there was no more disturbance that night.

So the haunting went on, night after night for two months. In his article John Wesley described many incidents, each as puzzling and inexplicable as the last. Here in his own words is one:

My father and mother had just gone to bed, and the candle was not taken away, when they heard three blows, and a second and a third three, as it were a large wooden staff struck upon a chest which stood by the bedside. My father immediately arose, put on his nightgown, and, hearing great noises below, took the candle and went down; my mother walked by his side. As they went down the broad stairs, they heard as if a vessel full of silver was poured upon my mother's breast and ran jingling down to her feet. Quickly after, there was a sound as if a large iron bell were thrown among many bottles under the stairs; but nothing was hurt.

Soon after, our large mastiff dog came, and ran to shelter himself between them. While the disturbances continued he used to bark and leap, and snap on one side and the other, and that frequently before any person in the room heard any noise at all. But after two or three days he used to tremble, and creep away before the noise began. And by this the family knew it was at hand; nor did the observation ever fail.

A little before my father and mother came into

the hall, it seemed as if a very large coal was violently thrown over the floor and dashed all in pieces; but nothing was seen.

My father then cried out, 'Sukey [Mrs Wesley's name, as well as one of her daughter's] do you not hear? All the pewter is thrown about the kitchen.'

But when they looked all the pewter stood in its place.

Then there was a loud knocking at the back door. My father opened it but saw nothing. It was then at the front door. He opened that, but it was lost labour. After opening first one, then the other, several times, he turned and went up to bed. But the noises were so violent all over the house that he could not sleep till four in the morning.

Several clergymen advised Samuel to leave the house. He never would. 'No!' he always replied, 'let the devil flee from me. I will never flee the devil.'

To the old minister the noises were nothing less than agents of evil attempting to strike fear into the hearts of a good Christian family. He was a man of iron will and clearly of great courage, for whatever others may think about the cause of the strange events at Epworth Parsonage, Samuel Wesley and the rest of his family were convinced the cause was not natural but supernatural.

Emilia Wesley later wrote, 'A whole month was

sufficient to convince anybody of the reality of the thing.' And from the way John Wesley wrote his account it is certain that he too believed there was more to the haunting of his home than the work of a trickster, or the echoing sound of the wind in the eaves, or the eerie creaking of a large house in the candle-lit silence of the night.

CHAPTER FIVE

The Man Who Gambled with the Devil

Glamis Castle belongs to the Earls of Strathmore. Princess Margaret was born there, and it is famous as the place where Macbeth is said to have murdered the Scottish King Duncan in AD 1040. A sword and a shirt of mail which are supposed to have belonged to Macbeth are on show at the castle which is steeped in history and legend. For many years people called it 'the most haunted house in Britain'. My favourite story of the haunting of Glamis is the one about the man who gambled with the Devil.

Many, many years ago in the days when great and wealthy gentlemen got drunk during dinner and had to be carried to bed by their servants, Glamis was owned by the notorious Earl Patie. Patie was such a loose-living man, loving all the pleasures of life and enjoying them to the full, that people called him 'The Wild Lord of Glamis'. But the pleasure that Earl Patie indulged in most of all was gambling. He gambled night and day with anyone he could persuade to chance their luck at cards. If his friends refused, he would call for the servants or the stable hands and order them to play.

No one willingly matched themselves against the Earl because all the time he gambled he drank glass after glass of whisky. The longer he played the drunker he grew, and the drunker he grew the shorter became his temper. If he lost, he would accuse his partner of cheating, and anyone foolish enough to argue was challenged to a duel.

It happened that late one cold and stormy November night the wild lord sat alone drinking heavily. He called for the cards and demanded that someone join him for a game. None of the Earl's family would do so. Neither would the servants. It was the Sabbath, they said, and not a day for gambling. The Earl was furious. He sent for his chaplain and commanded him to deal the cards. The chaplain not only refused, he forbade anyone else in the castle, family or servants, to join in the game. Cards, said the chaplain, were 'the Devil's bricks', an evil to be shunned.

Patie flew into a terrible rage. He cursed the chaplain, the servants, his family. Grabbing the cards he staggered drunkenly up the stairs, swearing oaths and insults.

'If no one else will play,' he bellowed, 'I'll invite the Devil himself to a game.'

Not long after he had settled himself in his room, Patie heard a loud knocking on his door. A deep voice called from the landing, asking if he still wished for a game.

'Yes,' roared the Earl, 'enter, whoever you are, in the foul fiend's name!'

The door was pushed open by a tall dark stranger, muffled in a heavy black cloak, his face hidden in the shadow cast by the brim of a huge black hat. The stranger nodded arrogantly, strode over to the table and sat down opposite the wild lord.

Delighted, Patie shuffled the cards. The stranger watched, smiling. Then he suggested an enormous stake. Patie hesitated. He had never risked such a sum before, and he doubted if he could pay should he lose. But his hesitation soon passed in his desire to gamble.

'I shall not lose,' he boasted. 'No one wins against me. Deal the cards.'

'But if I should win,' said the stranger, 'and you cannot pay your debt, you must agree to write a bond for anything of yours that I ask.'

'Done!' Patie replied, thumping the table in excitement. This would be a game worth playing!

Soon the servants heard violent shouts and curses drifting down from the Earl's room. Curious to know who had dared join their master, they crept to his door and listened. The Earl's voice they could recognize easily enough; but the other was unknown to them. Who could the visitor be? And how did he get into the house? None of them knew.

The game grew faster and more furious, the voices louder, more violent, more angry. And then came a drunken howl. Patie had lost. The servants heard the deep voice demanding a bond. An argument started, raged in loud confusion, ended with Patie pleading for one more game, one chance to win back his bond.

At this the butler could resist his curiosity no longer. Stooping down, he put an eye to the keyhole and peered into the room. No sooner had he done so than there was a blinding flash of light. The butler let out a cry of agony that echoed round the castle, fell backwards and collapsed to the floor. Round the eye he had placed to the keyhole was a bright yellow circle.

The servants had no time to tend the butler. Before any of them could collect their thoughts, the Earl threw open his door and rushed out threatening all manner of punishments for anyone who dared spy on him again. Commanding them to stay where they were, he turned back into the room to continue the game. But his opponent had gone. And with him the bond Earl Patie had signed only a moment before.

Patie was beside himself. He ordered the servants to search every room. Every corner, every possible hiding place, every way of escape was examined and examined again. Not a trace of the dark stranger could be found. Quite sober, his face deathly white, Patie was afraid for the first time in his life. He was quite sure now who his visitor had been, and he trembled to think of the bond he had sealed with his own signature. In his drunken desire to gamble, and thinking the stranger was merely playing a joke, he had signed away his soul.

As they left the room, the servants remembered the stunned butler. He was lying where they had left him, bruised and shocked, but conscious. In hushed tones Patie told them what had happened. He was sitting at play when the stranger suddenly threw down his cards and said in a loud voice firm with authority, 'Smite that eye!' Even as the stranger spoke, a flash of lightning darted across the room and struck the keyhole through which the unfortunate butler was peering.

From this time on Earl Patie was a changed man. Nervous, brooding, rarely gay, he lived as one under sentence of death. Five years later he died. Thereafter, every November of every year on Sunday nights the dead Earl's room was filled with eerie noises that echoed through the castle. People said it was the sound of the Earl's ghost gambling once more with the Devil, wrangling this time to retrieve his soul. The household put up with the annual haunting for many years. But at last it became so disturbing to everyone who lived in Glamis that the room was bricked up. Since then the gambling ghosts have been heard no more.

CHAPTER SIX

Haunted Hotels

Hotels: temporary homes for travellers, hiding places for the hunted, resting places for the weary, meeting places for the innocent and the criminal. Many are old buildings which for decades have given shelter to journeying strangers. It is scarcely surprising that almost every old hotel in the land has its ghost story to tell.

The Garrick's Head Hotel stands next to the old Theatre Royal in Bath. Once connected by a secret passage, the hotel and theatre share a ghost between them.

When the Garrick's Head was a private house years and years ago, a woman threw herself from the window above what is now the public bar. She died from her fall and her ghost has been seen many times since by visitors and by actors performing in the theatre.

She is called the 'grey lady', and she sits in one of the most expensive boxes watching the performance on stage. She has even been blamed for playing an amusing trick. A grandfather clock was used as part of the scenery on stage during a play. The clock did not go, of course. But suddenly, at just the wrong moment in the middle of the play, it was heard to chime. The actors said the grey lady had done it; but apart from this piece of mischief, she is a friendly enough spectator.

The grey lady is not the only ghost to haunt the Garrick's Head. Nor is this surprising, for at one time it was a gambling den run by a dashing and famous character called the Beau Nash. When the place was raided by the authorities, he and his clients used to escape through the secret passage into the theatre next door. Perhaps the ghosts are the uneasy spirits of some of the Beau's shady pals, one or two of whom were killed in drunken brawls, arguing about their winnings. Whoever the ghosts are, they cause some odd things to happen.

One Sunday only a few years ago, at about quarter past twelve, the landlord was standing behind the bar when the heavy cash-register lifted itself (or was it lifted by unseen hands?) off the counter and crashed to the floor, smashing a chair as it fell. No one was near the till at the time, and there was no natural explanation for its behaviour. Except, of course, the well-known ghosts!

On another occasion a party was being held in the hotel when a glass was seen to fly through the air and fall without breaking. The merry-making came to an astonished end.

Then there is the ghost who has been both seen and heard as he entered the secret passage – now blocked up. He was a heavily-built man wearing Regency-style clothes and a long brown wig that fell in curls to his shoulders. As he walked his feet made a squeaky sound. The sight was witnessed by the landlord's son. He thought at first that the man might be an actor from the theatre, dressed in costume for a play. When he looked into the passage, however, the figure had gone, and, what surprised him most, there were no footprints in the thick dust that covered the passage floor. When the landlord's son walked down the passage he left behind a trail of clear footprints which marked his path.

The same landlord who saw his till inexplicably crash to the floor also reported that twice, as he went through the cellar to tend his beer barrels, something stroked the back of his head. Cobwebs perhaps, brushing against him as he passed? There were none to be seen. It is also in the cellar that people have smelt a strong perfume unlike anything used by women in the hotel. Could this be the grey lady again? Or is it the perfume once used by the women who, it seems, began the hauntings in the Garrick's Head?

One night, when the place was still a private house, two men fought a duel with swords in what is now the public bar. Both men loved the same woman, and they argued about whose wife she should be. The beautiful cause of the trouble, the woman herself, knew which of the men she preferred. But the rivals were determined to settle the question between themselves and to their own satisfaction. It was a noisy, vicious battle; and as they fought in the downstairs room, the woman stood in her bedroom above listening to the quarrel and the clash of the swords beneath.

At last, one man slew the other. But the man who died was the man the woman loved. The victor ran up the stairs to claim the prize. But his heady success was short-lived. In the agony of her distress, the woman locked her door and hanged herself in her room before the suitor could break in and save her.

Perhaps it is the footsteps of this unhappy woman which can be heard from time to time in various parts of the house. Or is it the sorrowing spirit of the man who loved her, and died fighting a duel for her hand? Whatever the answer, the ghostly inmates of the Garrick's Head Hotel sometimes get into the newspapers. John Duller is only one of the many journalists who have stayed at the hotel hoping to see and hear something of the spectres. In Mr Duller's case, the ghosts came as something of a shock, for he did not know beforehand that the hotel was haunted. Here is part of what Mr Duller wrote about his visit in the *Western Daily Press* dated July 5th, 1963:

'I can vouch for loud and mysterious bumps in the night. It happened when I was staying in the pub two months ago, *before* I heard the story of the ghost. Several thuds woke me as I was dozing in the first-floor sitting-room. I searched the room and the corridor outside for ten minutes. But I found nothing except that the sounds seemed to have come from behind the panelling in a corner of the room.'

Half across England from the Garrick's Head, Bath, is another old public house, also known for a legendary haunting. The Ferry Boat Inn at Holywell in Huntingdonshire is said to stand on the spot where one Juliet Tousley died a sad death. She was a beautiful nineteen-year-old girl who loved a woodcutter named Tom Zoul. Tom courted Juliet, but in an off-hand way. He paid her too little attention, perhaps did not flatter her enough – for beautiful young girls like to be told they are beautiful, especially by the men they love. Juliet grew tired of Tom's bad behaviour and one day picked a quarrel, accusing him of neglecting her. Tom's anger was goaded by this. In the heat of the moment he said unkind things, even though, when all was said and done, he loved Juliet deeply.

Juliet was so hurt and upset by Tom's harsh words, so much did they rankle her, that in a fit of spite and pique she hanged herself from a willow tree that grew among the reeds on the bank of the River Ouse near Holywell.

'The spectre ... walks down to the
riverside and vanishes ...'

Poor Tom himself discovered her body next day. In deep distress he helped the villagers cut down his dead, beloved Juliet, and bury her in a grave by the waterside, dressed as she died in her best pink gown. They marked the grave with a roughly cut stone.

All this happened long ago, in the year 1050. But now, the story goes, Juliet walks in ghostly form once a year, on the anniversary of her tragic death, each March 17th. On that day people gather at the Ferry Boat Inn hoping to glimpse the spectre as it rises from the stone in the bar, that same stone laid by Tom Zoul over the body of his lover. And when the spectre has risen, it walks out of the inn, down to the riverside and there vanishes from view for another year. It is, they say, a pitiful sight: the lovelorn girl sorrowing still for the handsome woodcutter from whom she rashly separated herself in a moment of self-pity.

Of all the tales of haunted hotels none are more strange or more gruesome than the ones told about the White Garter in Portsmouth. Long ago such dreadful crimes were committed there that troubled spirits have disturbed it ever since. Three times the building has been pulled down and rebuilt in an effort to free the place of its ghosts. And each time the ghosts have returned to haunt the spot where they died.

Most famous of the stories of the White Garter Hotel is the one concerning a certain Mr Hamilton in the 1790s. He served in the Navy and was ordered to Portsmouth to be shipped overseas. When he arrived, he found the town packed with visitors, and with sailors just paid off from their ships. Everywhere the hotels and boarding houses were full.

Mr Hamilton searched all day long trying to find a lodging for the night, without success. At last, tired and dispirited, he discovered the White Garter, a seedy-looking hotel up an alleyway. The landlady offered him a bed, so long as he was willing to share with someone else, for there were two beds in the room and she did not want to lose business when trade was so good. As he did not like the idea of sharing with a stranger, Hamilton made a bargain. He would take the room for himself and pay for both beds, if the landlady would agree not to let the second bed to anyone else. The bargain was accepted and Mr Hamilton was shown to the room.

He was exceedingly tired after his long day spent tramping round the town, so he wasted no time in preparing for bed. Portsmouth was a less safe place then than it is now and before climbing between the sheets, he carefully locked the door. It was not long before he fell asleep.

So he remained for about an hour, then a noise in the alleyway roused him. He turned over to settle himself again and saw, by the light of the moon shining faintly through the window, someone lying slumped on the second bed. Mr Hamilton pushed himself up onto his elbow the clearer to see the figure. It was a man, dressed only in his trousers, and with a red handkerchief tied round his head. He was lying on the edge of the bed farthest from Mr Hamilton, his feet on the floor and the rest of him sprawled on his side across the bed. He seemed to be fast asleep.

Mr Hamilton was very angry to think that the landlady had broken her agreement after all. For a moment he considered waking his new companion and asking him to leave. But on second thoughts he decided this was not the best thing to do. The fellow looked like a sailor, heavily built and burly. It might be wise to avoid trouble at this time of night. Besides, the man was quiet and causing no bother. After watching him for a while, Mr Hamilton lay down once more and went off to sleep.

The sun was shining brightly through the window when next he woke. At once he looked at the other bed. The man was still there, lying just as Mr Hamilton had first seen him. And now, in the early morning light, he had a better chance to observe him closely.

The face was dark-skinned and handsome enough, but it was framed by unusual bushy black whiskers, thick and long. And what Mr Hamilton had taken by the light of the moon to be a red handkerchief, he now saw to his horror was a white cloth saturated with blood.

The shock set Mr Hamilton thinking. He wondered, for the first time, how the stranger had got into the room. There was only the one door, and he had locked it carefully before going to bed. It was in the centre of the wall between the two beds. Mr Hamilton went and checked that it was still secured. It was; and the key was in the lock, just where he had left it the night before. No one could possibly have got in without waking Mr Hamilton, for the lock would have had to be forced.

Mr Hamilton determined to have the matter out with the sleeping sailor. He turned to wake him up. The stranger had disappeared. Mr Hamilton could not believe his eyes. He had heard nothing, been only seconds inspecting the door and the lock. How could the fellow have got up without him hearing? How could he have left the room? A man apparently wounded, at that! There had been neither time nor way for escape.

Mr Hamilton searched the room for some sign or clue to what had happened. He looked under the beds, sounded the walls for secret doors or hiding places, looked behind the curtains that draped the windows, checked the window itself. Nothing. Not a hint to explain how the man got away.

Disturbed, Mr Hamilton dressed as quickly as he could and went downstairs to tackle the landlady about the affair. He found himself first up, and it was some time before the landlady came in.

He greeted the woman as calmly as he could, and asked at once for his bill. He could not, he said, stay a minute longer in the hotel after the landlady had allowed someone else to use his room.

'What do you mean?' the landlady said, blushing angrily. 'You took the room and had it alone. It is a comfortable room, too – there's not a better in all Portsmouth. I could have let the second bed four or five times over last night, but refused. Are you trying to cheat me? And you call yourself a gentleman!'

The woman was becoming hysterical and causing an embarrassing scene. To cut matters short, Mr Hamilton took out his wallet and gave the landlady twice what he had agreed to pay.

'I'm not complaining about the man who slept in my room,' he said as he did so, 'for he has given me no trouble. It was your breach of our agreement that annoyed me. Perhaps, however, you are not to blame,' he went on, trying to pacify the agitated woman, for she was growing more excited at every word he spoke. 'Probably one of your staff let the second bed, unaware of the bargain we struck.'

'What man?' demanded the landlady. 'There was nobody in your room, unless you let him in yourself.

You had the key, and I heard you lock the door behind you last night. If a man got in, you must have let him in yourself. For no one else did.'

'It is quite true that I locked my door,' said Mr Hamilton, picking up his luggage, 'but there was certainly a man, a sailor I took him to be, in my room last night. But I know no more about how he got in or out than I know where he got his broken head or his enormous whiskers.'

With that, Mr Hamilton walked towards the hotel door, hoping to escape further argument. But the landlady rushed to him and stopped him before he had taken more than a few steps. She was aghast: the angry flush had left her face which was now deathly white.

'Whiskers?' she said.

'Yes,' answered Mr Hamilton, puzzled at the turn of events. 'I never saw such a splendid pair in my life.'

'And a broken! . . .' stammered the landlady. 'For Heaven's sake, sir, come back a moment, I beseech you. Let me ask you to describe in every detail who and what you saw in your room last night.'

Mr Hamilton allowed himself to be led out of hearing of other guests, and then went through his story, relating just what had happened without exaggeration.

'I saw no one else, madam, but the sailor of whom I've just told you,' he ended, still confused by the change that had come over the landlady. 'I presume he took refuge in my room after a drunken fight, in order to sleep off the effects of his liquor. Though how he got in, or, more curious still, how he got out I cannot so much as guess.'

'Lord have mercy upon me!' cried the landlady, more agitated than before. 'It's all true, and the house is ruined for ever!'

'Come, come, madam, compose yourself,' said Mr Hamilton. 'What is the matter? Won't you tell me?'

At first, she would not. But Mr Hamilton was now determined to know what could cause such distress. Gradually the landlady controlled herself, and, after making Hamilton swear solemnly that he would tell her secret to no one, she poured out the troubles that were preying on her.

Three nights before Mr Hamilton arrived, some sailors had been drinking in the public bar. Some marines had come in, and soon a quarrel had broken out between the two parties. At first the argument was merely noisy, but before long the men grew violent. The landlady tried to interfere, but succeeded only in making matters worse.

At the height of the row, a marine picked up a beer mug and hit one of the sailors a sharp blow on the temple. The sailor was a strongly-built man, about twenty-five years old, and the most athletic-looking of the group. Nevertheless the blow knocked him senseless to the ground where he lay with blood streaming from his wound.

The argument ended at once. The marines fled. The sailors went to the aid of their stricken friend. But nothing they did brought him back to consciousness, nor could they stem the bleeding. The landlady began to fear trouble if other customers or, worse, the police came in. At her suggestion, the young man was carried to an upstairs room. There, a few minutes later, the sailor died as he lay sprawled across the bed.

What were they to do now? If the police discovered the death, questions would be asked that would be difficult to answer. All of them: marines, sailors, the landlady herself would be involved in a murder charge.

The sailors suggested that the best thing to do was to bury their friend in the hotel garden, and never to mention the dreadful business again. There was, they said, little likelihood of their friend being looked for, because he had just been discharged from his ship.

The landlady, frightened out of her wits and glad of any solution to her difficulties, was only too willing to agree to the plan. And so, in the dead of night, the sailor's body was buried in a hastily-dug grave in the garden at the back of the hotel.

'But then, sir,' said the landlady to Mr Hamilton as she wrung her hands in anguish, 'it's all of no use. Foul deeds will rise to smart the strongest conscience.

I shall never again dare to put anyone in your room, for there the poor young man was carried and there he died. They took off his jacket and waistcoat, and tied his wound with a cloth, but they could not stop the bleeding. As sure as you're standing there alive the dead has come back to haunt me.'

There was nothing to be done. Mr Hamilton racked his brain for some comfort to offer the poor woman, but he was so astonished by what he had heard he could think of nothing. Quietly he left the hotel and its distraught landlady. The poor woman had suffered enough and would suffer more in time to come. There was little point in adding to her trouble by informing the police.

Next day he sailed for the Mediterranean and did not set foot in England again for fifteen years. When at last he came home, he went to Portsmouth intending to look up the landlady at the White Garter and discover how she had fared while he had been away. He combed the area but could find no trace of the hotel. New buildings stood where it should have been.

So the White Garter Hotel disappeared, with its history of murders and hauntings. Even so, people still claim that ghosts are to be seen at the spot where the hotel once stood.

CHAPTER SEVEN

The Mannington Ghost

Mannington Hall stands near Corpusty, a small village in Norfolk, and is the site of a very strange haunting indeed. The ghostly happenings were witnessed by Dr Augustus Jessop, once headmaster of Norwich Grammar School, who recorded his experiences in a magazine, the *Athenaeum*, in January 1880.

Dr Jessop was interested in old books, and his friend, Lord Orford, who owned Mannington Hall, had a rare collection, including some which Dr Jessop especially wanted to see. So it was arranged that he should visit the Hall and spend some time going through the library.

He arrived at the fifteenth-century mansion about four o'clock one afternoon. He dined that evening with his host and five other guests. After a most convivial and entertaining meal the company played cards. At half-past ten two of the guests had to leave, and the others decided to go to bed. Dr Jessop, however, was anxious to see the old books which so much interested him and asked if he might sit up late and study them. He was led into a comfortable room next to the library. A fire burned brightly in the grate, there was a table to work at, and a tray of drinks stood ready for his refreshment. Here he was left to his work.

He went at once into the library to search for the books he wanted, and found them high on a top shelf. He brought a chair to stand on and lifted them down. There were six volumes altogether. He carried them into the reading-room where he settled himself at one corner of the table with the fire on his left, and the books in a pile on his right. By eleven o'clock he was hard at work.

For two hours Dr Jessop read, totally absorbed in the rare volumes. He took each one in turn, read from it, took notes about it, and, when he had finished, placed it in a second pile in front of him. That done he would get up and stir the fire – he was a chilly person and liked warmth – before taking up the next book from the unread pile at his right hand. In this way he got along much more quickly than he had expected. By one o'clock he had finished with all but one of the six books. Before he began work on it, he had a drink, wound his watch and thought to himself that by two o'clock he would be in bed. Pleased at the way things were going and delighted with what he had found in the books, he settled himself to tackle the last volume.

Half an hour later he was nearing the end of his task when he became aware of a large white hand

*'He was bending over the table and seemed to
be examining the pile of books . . .'*

within twelve inches of his right elbow. Turning his
head, Dr Jessop saw the figure of a tall man. He was
sitting at the table, bending over to examine the pile
of books in front of Dr Jessop. The man's face was only
half visible. Dr Jessop could see his closely-cut reddish-
brown hair, his ear, his clean-shaven cheek with high
cheekbones, the corner of his right eye, the side of his
forehead. He was dressed in some kind of priest's robe
made of thick silk-like material, fastened up to the
chin. Round the neck was a narrow rim about an inch

wide, of satin or velvet, standing up like a collar.

The man's right hand, the hand that Dr Jessop had first noticed, clasped the left lightly; blue veins rose under the white flesh.

The doctor gazed at the figure for some time, quite sure that it was not living. Thoughts rushed through his head, but he felt no unease or fear. In fact, he found himself intensely curious about the strange visitor. For a moment he thought of sketching the man, and he looked round for a pencil. Then he remembered that in his room upstairs he had a sketch book. He wondered whether he should go off as quietly as he could and bring it down. But the ghostly figure so fascinated him that he was afraid to stir in case he frightened it away.

Dr Jessop could never explain why he made his next move. Without thinking, he lifted his left hand from the paper, stretched it out to the pile of books in front of him, and took hold of the top one. His arm passed in front of the man as he did so. At once the figure disappeared. It did not walk or move. It simply vanished.

At this, Dr Jessop coolly returned to his work. For another five minutes he went on writing as though nothing had happened. He had reached the last few words left to be written when the ghost appeared again, exactly as it had before.

Dr Jessop saw the hands close to his own, and

turned his head to examine the spectre more closely. He wanted very much to say something, and formed a sentence in his head. But when he opened his mouth to speak, he found he dared not utter a word. He was afraid to hear the sound of his own voice. And so there sat the ghost, bending over the books, and beside it sat Dr Jessop, speechless, fascinated.

At last the doctor turned back to his notes and wrote the final two or three words. Looking at these same words later, he could see not one sign that they had been written under such unusual circumstances: the writing was just as calm and normal as the words he had set down before the ghost appeared. Having finished his task, he shut the book, threw it on to the table in front of him. As it fell it made a slight noise. The ghost vanished.

Dr Jessop leaned back in his chair and for some minutes stared at the fire, trying to collect his thoughts. And all the time he was wondering whether the ghost would come again. If it did, would it hide the fire from him with its body? Or would he see the flames shining through the spectral shape? Now, for the first time, he felt that he was losing his nerve. So he stood up, lit his candle ready for bed, picked up the books and went into the library. There he replaced five of the volumes. But he brought the sixth back into the reading-room and put it on the table at the spot where he had been writing.

The doctor does not say why he did this. Perhaps he felt that as this was the book that seemed to interest the ghost, it would be a friendly act to leave it where the ghost could come and see it again. Whatever caused the doctor to leave the book on the table we cannot know; but having done so all uneasiness left him. He blew out the candles that lit the room and went off to bed. He slept soundly until morning.

Many people have offered explanations for what Dr Jessop saw: that it was an hallucination, a dream, a trick played on him. But no one can know for sure. The man to whom it all happened was wise: he described the experience but never tried to explain it away. For the rest of his life it remained for him a treasured and fascinating mystery.

CHAPTER EIGHT

The Ghostly Skulls of Calgarth Hall

Kraster and Dorothy Cook owned a small farm over-looking Lake Windermere in Westmorland. They worked hard, lived simply, and were happy.

All the land round their farm was owned by a wealthy man, Myles Phillipson by name. He was a friend of the local gentry, he held the position of magistrate for the area, he possessed great riches, and yet he still had one ambition. He wished to build for himself and his family a magnificent new house which was to impress his friends and display his wealth.

Now on all the Phillipson's land there was no spot half so beautiful or suitable for a new house as the site on which stood Kraster Cook's small cottage. It over-looked the lake, giving a wonderful view of the water and the fells beyond.

Phillipson tried many times to persuade Kraster and Dorothy to sell their farm. Each time they re-fused. The bid was increased; bigger and bigger sums of money were offered, amounts Phillipson thought only fools would refuse. But the Cooks valued something more than money: their happiness on the farm they loved. At last Phillipson's thwarted ambition turned sour. He would, he swore, possess the Cooks' farm by hook or by crook, whether the farmer was alive or dead.

It was his beautiful wife who put into the powerful landowner's mind the plan that eventually brought disaster to all the Phillipson family.

A week before Christmas Phillipson visited the Cooks' cottage. He was charming and friendly. He had decided, he said, to build his new house on his own land. He could see the Cooks were determined not to sell. And who could blame them? No one would willingly move from such a perfect place! He hoped that Dorothy and Kraster would let bygones be bygones, forget the angry words of the past, and remain friends. To show his goodwill, Phillipson invited them to dinner on Christmas Day.

Of course, Dorothy and Kraster were delighted to hear their powerful and influential neighbour had given up the idea of buying their land. But they did not want to accept the invitation to Christmas dinner. They would feel out of place and uncomfortable in such company as would be present. However, to show their renewed friendship and so as not to offend Phillipson, they politely accepted.

Christmas Day came and Dorothy and Kraster were in a nervous sweat at the thought of their visit. They dressed themselves as best they could and set off for the Phillipson mansion. When they arrived, they were almost tongue-tied with embarrassment. Everyone else was dressed in fine clothes, while Kraster and Dorothy wore the heavy rough things which were all they could afford. Their host and hostess tried hard to put them at their ease; but it was no use. Dorothy and Kraster stumbled and stammered, and finally sat awkwardly with the other guests, speaking only when they were spoken to, and then saying very little.

Dinner was served. In the dining-room the long table gleamed with silver and glass and the best china. Opposite Kraster stood a magnificent golden bowl, glittering in the candlelight. The poor farmer, as much to avoid conversation as to admire its beauty, stared at the precious object as he ate.

After a while there came a pause in the conversation. Out of the silence Mrs Phillipson said loudly to Kraster, 'I see you are admiring that bowl, Mr Cook. It is indeed worth looking at!'

Kraster mumbled some appropriate reply, blushing with embarrassment as every eye in the room was turned on him. Other guests then commented on the beauty and value of the ornament before the conversation passed on to different subjects.

When dinner was finished, the guests went off into other rooms to dance and talk and play Christmas

party games. But not Dorothy and Kraster. They had
had enough. They waited about in the dining-room
until a polite moment came when they could take
their leave. Free at last from the ordeal, they walked
back with glad relief to their own, familiar surroundings.

They were not free or left in familiar surroundings
for long. Next day a troop of soldiers marched up to
the farmhouse. They had orders, they said, to arrest
Dorothy and Kraster. Without any delay or explanation, the bewildered couple were carried off to jail
and locked in separate cells.

For a week they never saw each other, nor were they
allowed to communicate. They next met, confused
and shocked, in court. Only then did they learn why
they had been arrested. They were accused of stealing
a golden bowl, the property of Myles Phillipson.

It was on the order of the local magistrate that they
had been arrested. It was the local magistrate who tried
them now. That magistrate was Myles Phillipson.

The first and chief witness was Myles Phillipson's
wife. She swore that the stolen bowl had been on the
table during Christmas dinner in her house. Kraster
Cook, she said, sat opposite the bowl, and had gazed at
it throughout the meal. Indeed, went on Mrs Phillipson, she had mentioned the bowl to him during
dinner, and many other guests had heard the conversation.

Some of the guests were called to the witness box. Each one supported Mrs Phillipson's testimony.

Then came two servants from the Phillipson household. They swore that they had seen the Cooks lingering in the dining-room while the other guests were dancing after dinner.

The bowl itself was exhibited. Two soldiers from the party that arrested Dorothy and Kraster gave evidence that after the arrest they searched the Cooks' farm cottage. They had found the bowl hidden in the bedroom.

The magistrate asked the prisoners if they had anything to say in their own defence. Dumbfounded by the evidence, the farmer and his wife could do nothing but mutter a denial of the charge against them.

In those days theft was punishable by death. So it was that Myles Phillipson, Magistrate, could and did sentence Dorothy and Kraster Cook to be hanged by their necks until they were dead.

Only now did Dorothy Cook find strength and words to speak. In a loud voice that echoed round the courtroom, eyes wild with righteous indignation, finger pointing at the magistrate, she cried out:

'Look out for yourself, Myles Phillipson. You think you have done a fine thing. But the tiny lump of land you lust for is the dearest a Phillipson has ever bought or stolen. You will never prosper, nor any of your breed. Whatever scheme you undertake will wither in your hand. Whatever cause you support will always lose. The time will come when no Phillipson will own an inch of land. And while Calgarth walls shall stand, we will haunt it night and day. You will never be rid of us!'

Dorothy was dragged from court. A few days later she and her beloved husband died on the gallows. Their bodies were still swinging from the gibbet at the crossroads when the Phillipsons took possession of their farmhouse, pulled it down, and began building the sumptuous house they had longed for: Calgarth Hall.

By the following Christmas, the new house was ready. Myles Phillipson and his wife held a great banquet on Christmas Day to celebrate. And it was then that Dorothy's curse began to come true.

Guests crowded into the new Hall, admiring, envying the owners, impressed by such a show of wealth and social position. The dinner was boisterously merry. In the middle of it, Mrs Phillipson left the table to fetch a jewel that she wanted her guests to admire.

These were the days before electric or even gas lighting: the rooms and stairs of Calgarth Hall were lit by candles that threw deep shadows which danced when draughts stirred the candle flames. But these things meant nothing to Mrs Phillipson, she was used to them. And Dorothy's curse was long since forgotten, if it was ever thought of at all.

As Mrs Phillipson turned a corner in the dimly-lit stairs, she came on something that made her blood run cold, her eyes stare in terrified amazement. She stopped dead in her tracks, for a moment unable to utter a sound or move another step.

No more than inches in front of her, resting on the wide banisters so near she could have reached out and touched them, were two grinning skulls. From one, hair streamed down in wispy strands. And both seemed about to open their grinning mouths to speak.

With a scream, Mrs Phillipson recovered her senses, turned and fled. Whimpering in terror, she ran in to the startled dinner party; trembling, white, and stammering, she gasped out what she had just seen.

Phillipson at once grabbed up a sword and a candle. Others of the men did so too. Together they ran to the stairs. The skulls were still there.

Even the men were shaken by the sight. They too stopped in their tracks. For a moment no one moved or said a word. Then one of the men, bolder than the others, went cautiously up to the skulls and thrust at them with his sword. They were real enough. The sword rang as it struck solid bone.

'Someone is playing a trick,' shouted Phillipson, livid with anger.

There and then he set about questioning the servants. For some reason one of the houseboys was suspected. He denied having anything to do with the skulls. Phillipson did not believe him and ordered the boy to be taken to the cellar and left there, tied to a pillar, until he confessed.

The skulls were picked up on a sword blade and thrown into the courtyard.

There was no more merry-making that Christmas night at Calgarth Hall. The party broke up. Guests who lived nearby went home; the others retired to bed.

About two o'clock in the morning, the household was woken by a number of anguished screams. A crowd of tousled guests gathered round Myles Phillipson on the landing outside the bedrooms. The screams came from the staircase. Bunched together, fearful of what they would find, the startled group crept cautiously to the stairs.

What they saw struck deeper terror into them than anything they had seen before, or wished to see again. Perched on a step, gleaming in an eerie light, were the two grinning skulls.

No one slept again that night. When dawn came, Myles Phillipson himself took the dreadful objects and threw them into a pond.

This was but the beginning. Next night from behind locked doors all over the house came the chilling screams. And next morning the two skulls were found once more on the stairs. So it was night after night. No matter what was done to rid the Hall of the skulls – burying, or burning, or smashing with hammers – always the following night those ghastly screams, and the skulls found on the stairs!

One by one the servants left the house. Phillipson's friends, remembering Dorothy's curse, refused invitations to stay at Calgarth. Nor would they have the Phillipsons in their own homes. For Dorothy's curse promised misfortune not on the Phillipsons only, but on all with whom they had to do.

Even so, Myles Phillipson and his wife refused to give up the house they had for so long set their hearts on owning. They remained, with their children, and suffered the nightly terror. If the skulls had been ghostly apparitions, perhaps people would have minded less. But they were not. They were tangible bone, solid images of death, fearsome reminders of the evil deeds on which Calgarth Hall was built. Every night as they climbed into bed the Phillipsons wondered when the time would come that the screams would wake them and they would open their eyes to find the grinning skulls there on the pillow beside them.

Meanwhile, just as Dorothy had promised, Myles Phillipson's business began to decline. No one would deal with him; everything he touched failed. Slowly his wealth dwindled. When at last he died, he left his

'*The two skulls jumped up onto the table*'

son with little fortune. And the skulls screamed ceaselessly all that night.

From the time of Phillipson's death, the skulls appeared only twice a year: on Christmas Day, the anniversary of the treacherous dinner; and on the day of the year on which Dorothy and Kraster were hanged. Even so, the heir fared little better than his father. Nothing prospered. Once he tried holding a party for his friends in his parents' old home. In the middle of dinner the dining-room doors were flung open. Across the floor rolled the two skulls, jumped up onto the table, and lay there gaping at the assembled guests.

So it went on, one heir succeeding the last, each one inheriting the dreadful curse, and each worse off than his father before him, until the family came to an end. The last member lived as an outcast and died a penniless beggar.

Thus was Dorothy's promise fulfilled. Calgarth Hall remains today, the Phillipson coat of arms still visible on one of the old fireplaces. But the house is peaceful now; the skulls haunt it no more.

CHAPTER NINE

Death's Drummer Boy

Cortachy Castle is an ancient Scottish fortress in the wilds of Angus, the home of the Ogilvies, and family seat of the Earls of Airlie. For many years a ghost has haunted the household, a drummer whose playing foretells the coming of a death in the family.

Many years ago, one of the Earls had a young drummer among his servants, a strong young man, handsome and charming and full of fun. Women could not resist him, and he enjoyed their attentions. It may be that even the Earl's wife lost her heart to the dashing young fellow. Whatever the cause, the Earl was very jealous. Many a time he hotly warned the servant of his behaviour with the women of the house. And once, in a fit of jealous rage, the Earl threatened the drummer's life. There followed a violent quarrel between master and servant, and the drummer told the Earl that if he ever carried out his threat, he, the drummer, would haunt the Ogilvies for ever afterwards.

The Earl cannot have believed him. For one night he and some of his men trapped the drummer in an

Cortachy Castle

upstairs room. They tied the young man's hands and feet, thrust his drum over his head, and threw him out of the window onto the stone paving below. The drummer died instantly.

Since that time, whenever a member of the Ogilvie family is near death – whether they know it or not – a ghostly drum is heard beating a tattoo in the castle or somewhere nearby on the estate.

Many people have heard that deathly warning. In 1844 a young lady, a Miss Dalrymple, was visiting

Cortachy. She was dressing for dinner on the night of her arrival when she heard coming from just below her window the faint sound of a drum. There was a hollowness, an unearthly quality in the sound that caught Miss Dalrymple's attention. The beating got louder. She looked out of the window to find out who was playing, but saw no one.

During dinner, Miss Dalrymple asked Lord Airlie during a pause in the conversation, 'My Lord, who is your drummer?'

The Earl turned pale and stopped eating. Lady Airlie also seemed upset. Everyone at the table sat in silent embarrassment. Miss Dalrymple could see that somehow she had said the wrong thing, and let the topic go by. After dinner, however, she took a younger member of the family aside and asked again about the drummer.

'What!' he said: 'Have you never heard of the drummer boy?'

'Never,' said Miss Dalrymple. 'Who is he?'

'Why,' said the young Ogilvie, 'he is a ghost who goes about the house playing his drum whenever there is to be a death in the family. The last time he was heard was shortly before the death of the Earl's first wife. That is why he turned so pale just now. It is a very unpleasant subject in this family, I assure you.'

Now it was Miss Dalrymple who felt upset. More

The ghostly drummer boy

than this, the idea of a ghost drumming his way round the castle frightened her somewhat. And when she heard him drumming again next day, she invented an excuse to leave Cortachy and return home.

Nearly six months later news came that Lady Airlie, the Earl's second wife, had died while on a trip to Brighton. By her side was a note saying she had known from the time Miss Dalrymple mentioned the drummer that he was tattooing her own death warning.

Five years later, on the evening of August 19th, 1849, a young Englishman was riding across the Forfarshire moors on his way to a shooting party on the Cortachy estate. It was already dark when the Englishman came in sight of the lighted windows of the shooting lodge. Just then, he heard the faint swelling sound of a band accompanied by a drum. The music seemed to be coming from a ridge of ground between the Englishman and the house. The rider reined in his horse and listened. The music grew louder, and the young man could not help feeling there was something eerie, unnatural about the sound. In a few moments, to his great relief, the music died away.

The Englishman rode on. It was when he arrived at the shooting lodge that he learned for the first time that his friend and host, the Earl's eldest son, had been called to London urgently. The Earl was dangerously ill. The following day, he died. The

Englishman's friend succeeded as the tenth Earl of Cortachy Castle. But like all the Ogilvies, he lived in dread of hearing the ghostly drummer beat out his mortal music.

CHAPTER TEN

The Nameless Horror of Berkeley Square

London's most famous nineteenth-century haunting took place in a house in fashionable Mayfair: at 50 Berkeley Square. For a time people used to come and stare at the building and speculate about the ghost – a ghost so horrible that the owner of the house left it deserted for many years.

Few who saw the ghost lived to tell the tale. Lord Lyttleton was one of the few who did. He belonged to a family who were called 'the most haunted family in England'. He collected ghosts. And he spent a night in the second-floor room at 50 Berkeley Square – the room where the ghost always appeared. He took with him two blunderbuss guns loaded with buckshot and sixpenny pieces. The silver coins were meant as charms to protect him from the evil spectre.

During the night Lord Lyttleton met the ghost. It came into the room and leapt through the air at him. In the nick of time, he managed to raise the gun and fire. The ghost fell like a shot duck to the floor, then seemed to evaporate. Lord Lyttleton could describe no more about the 'thing' he had seen, nothing about its looks and shape. It was merely a shadowy presence. But of this he was sure: he had never met a more terrible, more malign ghost in his life.

So famous was the Horror in its day that a now equally famous ghost story was based on it by a writer called Edward Bulwer-Lytton, who specialized in tales of the supernatural. But his hero suffers far worse at the hands of the spectre than Lord Lyttleton – or anyone else – suffered in the room in Berkeley Square.*

There are many accounts of the hauntings of this ghoulish ghost. The two best known concern Sir Robert Warboys and a couple of sailors.

Sir Robert was a handsome young man with an ancestral home at Bracknell in Berkshire. He did not believe in ghosts nor any supernatural spirits. When he heard of the terrible things people had endured at number 50 he dismissed them as impossible. He said as much to some friends one night. They argued, and finally challenged Sir Robert to spend a night alone in the haunted room. Sir Robert took up the challenge.

The owner of the house, Mr Benson, was contacted, and asked permission for Sir Robert to sleep in the second-floor bedroom. Mr Benson wanted nothing to do with the escapade; he knew, he said, what had been

* The story is called 'The Haunted and the Haunters', and can be found in *Ghosts*, a book of stories compiled by Aidan and Nancy Chambers (Macmillan Topliner).

the fate of others who had dared sleep there. But Sir Robert and his friends were determined. It was now a matter of honour: Sir Robert had been challenged and he had accepted. If Mr Benson would agree then they would all come to the house on the appointed night and be on hand to aid Sir Robert should he come to harm. Furthermore, Sir Robert would be armed with a gun. Surely these precautions would be safeguard enough against the worst of attackers – human or ghostly?

Reluctantly, Mr Benson agreed. A night was fixed for the visit. Sir Robert and his friends went off, excited by the prospect of taking part in such an unusual event.

The appointed evening came. The party met at Mr Benson's house and ate dinner together. They laughed and talked with forced good humour: everyone was nervous though they pretended not to be. Everyone, that is, except Mr Benson. He was nervous and did not try to hide it. Rather, he tried to persuade Sir Robert to give up this madcap idea. Sir Robert refused. His honour was at stake. Besides, he did not believe anything would – or even could – happen.

Rational argument was useless. So Mr Benson went once more through the safeguards. Sir Robert was to have a gun loaded and ready by his side in the room. His friends were to sit up throughout the night in case help was needed. Added to this, Mr Benson had arranged for a bell to be installed in the sitting-room where Sir Robert's friends were to wait. It was attached to a bell-pull in the haunted room. Should Sir Robert need help, he was to ring on the bell to warn his companions.

Sir Robert agreed to do this. But, he went on, he was feeling more nervous than he had expected. Therefore, he wanted everyone to wait until he rang the bell twice before coming to him.

Dinner over, the plans understood by everyone present, Sir Robert was shown to the room.

It was large and comfortably furnished with a double bed and armchairs. Two big windows looked out over the square. A fire was burning brightly in the hearth.

Sir Robert took off his jacket. As he did not expect to sleep that night, he propped himself up on the bed. At one side he had the pistol cocked and ready. On the other side hung the bell-pull.

In the room below, Mr Benson and Sir Robert's friends settled themselves for their night's vigil. One flight of stairs separated the two rooms.

Sir Robert had gone upstairs at quarter past eleven. Nothing happened until the twelve o'clock chimes rang through the city. As the last strokes of midnight sounded, the little bell on the sitting-room wall jangled. Mr Benson sprang from his chair and ran to the door.

'Wait,' cried one of the others. 'He said he would ring twice if he needed us.'

The words were hardly out of his mouth before the bell jangled violently, almost tearing itself free from the wall.

Benson rushed from the room closely followed by the others. Halfway up the stairs he heard a shot fired in the haunted room. Seconds later he threw open the door.

Sir Robert lay with his legs sprawled across the bed, his head hanging over the edge almost touching the floor. In his left hand he grasped the bell-pull, which had been torn from its fixing. On the floor near his right hand lay the pistol.

Benson and the others hurried across the room. It was then they saw Sir Robert's face. His eyes stared from their sockets in an agony of terror and fear. His lips were curled back over his teeth, which were clenched tightly as though locked in a fit.

'My God!' said one of the men. 'Cover him up.'

Benson lifted the fear-stiffened body onto the bed and draped it with a sheet.

Sir Robert had died, not from a bullet but from such extreme terror as no man can live through. What was it that could cause such deadly fear? No one knows. The spectre has been described as a man-ghost with an unbelievably ghastly face, a face white and flabby with a huge gaping mouth black as pitch. Others have said it was an animal creature with many legs and tentacles, a monstrous thing that crawled from London's sewers. Yet others say it was a shapeless being composed of depthless shadows.

On one thing only everyone agrees: it was an evil being that wished the death of any victim foolish enough or unfortunate enough to stray into its domain – that comfortably-furnished Mayfair room where Sir Robert gambled his life for his honour, and lost.

Edward Blunden and Robert Martin were two sailors who met the evil ghost by chance. They were on their way from Portsmouth to their homes. They arrived in London late on a December night with little money left in their pockets. For a time they wandered the streets arguing about where to spend the night. They were walking through Berkeley Square when they noticed a TO LET sign outside a dilapidated house. Had they but known, this was the infamous number 50. For forty years it had been empty; no one dared live in it.

To Blunden and Martin it seemed the answer to their problem. It would at least be a place to shelter and keep warm till morning. They got in by a basement window. One of them had a stump of candle in his pocket. This they lit, and by its light explored the downstairs rooms. All round were signs of neglect:

50 Berkeley Square

bits of furniture were scattered about, dust was every-where, rats scuttled across the floors.

They decided to climb up to the first floor and see what the rooms were like there. But again, all was ruin and disorder. So by the dwindling light of the almost exhausted candle, the two men climbed to the second floor.

Blunden was feeling nervous by this time, and wanted to leave the house. Martin would not hear of it. Why should they pay for a lodging, he said, when this place was cheap and good enough for a few hours!

At this moment they entered the haunted room. It was less disordered than the others and Martin decided a fire could be made in the hearth. Between them the sailors managed to collect some bits of wood and soon there was a warming blaze that cheered them up. They settled down for the night.

Martin went to sleep at once. Blunden felt uneasy and wakefully watched the fire as it flickered in the grate. And it was he who first heard the noise. He woke Martin with a vigorous shake.

'Listen,' he whispered.

At first Martin could hear nothing. But then came the sound of a footstep on the stairs. After a pause, the same sound again, but nearer this time. Then another step, nearer yet. And what made these footfalls more frightening than anything Martin had ever heard before was that they were not human. Not even anything earthly. They made a soft, hollow sound, but also they scratched on the bare wooden boards of the steps. Scratched as though the feet were padded and clawed like an animal's.

On the steps came with agonizing slowness; on and upwards. On, until they reached the door of the room where Martin and Blunden sat sweating from fear. And there they stopped.

Slowly the room door opened. Something came in, but Martin was hard put to it to know what that something was. A collection of shadows, perhaps? A shapeless form? A Being, no doubt of that!

Blunden screamed. Both men scrambled to their feet and faced the spectre which seemed to be growing in size as they watched.

, Frantic with fear, Blunden looked round desperately for something to defend himself with. An old curtain rod was propped against the wall near a window. He rushed to it, and grabbed it up.

As he did so the spectre moved so that it was placed between Blunden and the door. Then from out of its shapeless, featureless shadows emerged two limbs. Not hands or arms, quite. They reminded Martin of a huge bird's talons. For a moment the thing remained motionless, towering over Blunden, its 'limbs' outstretched. But then it began to move slowly, deliberately towards him.

He let out another anguished scream as he saw the thing coming towards him. But the spectre did not pause.

It was now that Martin saw his chance. As the ghost moved towards Blunden, the open door was left unguarded. Martin dived for it, tumbled out of the room, and crashed down the stairs. He could never remember undoing the bolts that secured the front door, but somehow he did, for that was the way he left the house. Panic-stricken, yelling for help, he ran from the square.

In Piccadilly he found a policeman. Almost demented, Martin stammered out some of his story as he brought the policeman back to Berkeley Square. As they were running towards the house both men heard the sound of breaking glass and splintering wood, and a long falling scream. Then silence.

They found Blunden's body crumpled over the basement steps. His neck was broken. And his eyes stared from his face in stark, paralysed horror.

No one has ever explained the ghost of 50 Berkeley Square. It is a nameless horror which for a time in the last century was the wonder and talk of London. It has gone now. The building stands in the busy square, disturbed only by the traffic that roars past its door.

CHAPTER ELEVEN

Sid Mularney's Ghost and other Poltergeists

'Poltergeist' is the name given to ghosts which make noises and throw things about, but are rarely seen. The name comes from two German words: *polter* meaning noise, and *geist* meaning ghost. Noise-ghost! In German fairy stories poltergeists are depicted as mischievous little gnomes who creep into people's houses and cause confusion. They rock chairs, smash dishes over each other's heads, make pictures fall off walls, throw stones at human beings and frighten horses so that they bolt. They even drop one another down wells and lie gurgling in the water until other poltergeists rescue them.

Real poltergeists are not usually so amusing to have around. The Epworth Parsonage haunting (Chapter 4) was the work of a poltergeist. And so were the strange goings-on in Sid Mularney's workshop.

Sid Mularney is a motorcycle dealer whose customers include well-known motorcycling champions. His shop is in Leighton Buzzard in Bedfordshire. The trouble started when he began expanding his premises. This is how the local newspaper, the *Leighton*

Buzzard Observer, reported the haunting, on May 28th, 1963:

When Leighton motorcycle dealer, Mr Sid Mularney, decided to extend his workshop by removing a partition, he was taking on more than he anticipated. For he is now certain that he offended a poltergeist.

Neighbours are blaming 'Mularney's Ghost' for weird noises that keep them awake at night, and Mr Mularney, who claims actually to have witnessed the poltergeist's pranks, is certain that the building in Lake Street, Leighton, is haunted.

It was about a fortnight ago when he decided to take down the partition in the workshop which houses racing-motorcycles used by the world champion rider, Mike Hailwood.

The following morning, said Mr Mularney, he went to the door, opened it, and found three bikes on the floor. The machines, which are used by local rider Dave Williams, had their fairings smashed.

A few days later Mr Mularney was working on a racing gearbox, and when he realized he couldn't finish it unless he worked late, he decided to stay on. And it wasn't until three o'clock that he finished.

As he was wiping his hands, weird things started to happen.

'I felt something rush by me. I looked round and

'Spanners flew off hooks'

spanners flew off hooks on the wall and a tarpaulin, covering a bike, soared into the air,' he declared.

'You would have to see it to believe it. I was scared stiff. I grabbed a hammer, got out of the room as fast as I could and made straight for home. My wife was asleep and I woke her up to tell her about it.'

Since then other peculiar things have been taking place, and neighbours have been complaining of weird noises at night.

Mrs Cynthia Ellis, proprietress of the Coach and

Horses Restaurant*, next door in Lake Street, said she had been woken during the night several times 'by strange bangings and clatterings'.

'I looked out of the window, but there was never anything there.'

She said her young son, Stephen, was first to wake up and hear noises.

'We thought it was just a child's imagination, but we soon changed our minds,' she said.

'The atmosphere round here has become very tense during the past fortnight. It's all very odd,' said Mrs Ellis.

Since his strange experience Mr Mularney has discovered odd happenings in the workshop. One morning he found a huge box of nuts and bolts 'too heavy to lift' scattered all over the floor. Since then he has discovered petrol tanks which have been moved about and even large bolts missing, which, he claims, he could never mislay.

Sid Mularney's shop used to be a basket-making factory and there is a story that someone is supposed to have hanged himself there. Perhaps when Mr Mularney removed the partition he disturbed the poor man's ghost. No one really knows, however, and for the past few years, Sid Mularney has gone about his business without any more trouble from the 'noise-ghost'.

* Now closed.

One of the earliest documents recording the activities of poltergeists, a book written by Alexander Telfair in 1696, describes in detail the haunting of a farm owned by Andrew Mackie in Ringcroft. In this case, the poltergeists eventually showed themselves.

The haunting began in February 1695. One morning Andrew Mackie found his cattle had been mysteriously let out of their shed during the night. The following night the same thing happened again, and this time one of the animals was tied from a beam in the shed so that its feet were just touching the ground.

Mackie thought someone was playing tricks on him so he set a watch to catch them. The guards never actually caught anybody, but they had plenty of excitement! Between February and April the Mackie family had stones thrown about in the farmhouse; they were pulled from their beds by invisible hands and pushed roughly to the floor; stones and wooden poles came for them and beat them out of the house.

Three men praying at a bedside first saw the ghost – or part of it. One of them wrote, 'I felt something thrusting my arm up, and casting my eyes thitherward perceived a little white hand and an arm, from the elbow down, but it vanished presently.'

The Mackie children went into the house one day and 'saw something like a person sitting by the fire with a blanket about it'. The youngest child must have had a lot of courage. He went straight up to the

H.H.—6

'something' and pulled the blanket away. Underneath there was nothing but a tall stool turned upside down.

Three months of such experiences were enough to convince everyone on Mackie's farm that their troubles were not caused by any human being, but by a poltergeist. In those days – as is still done today – haunted houses were exorcised. By prayers and ritual acts priests call on the ghosts to quit their haunts and leave the people who live there in peace. Sometimes the ghosts do as they are asked; sometimes they do not!

On April 5th, 1695, a group of ministers gathered at Mackie's farm intending to hold an exorcism. They did not get far. A hail of stones fell on them from all sides, driving them off. Some of those watching the service found themselves grabbed by the legs and held upside down in the air.

But perhaps the ministers were more successful than they thought. On April 26th a ghostly voice was heard. First of all it threatened to carry everyone off to Hell. Then it promised 'thou shalt be troubled till Tuesday'.

True to its word, on Tuesday night the people keeping watch in the barn saw a huge black shape gather in a corner. Slowly the shape increased in size until it was like an enormous black cloud. Suddenly this 'cloud' seemed to grab the people on watch by the arms and hold them so tightly the bruises hurt for five days afterward. Then the cloud vanished, never to visit Andrew Mackie's farm again.

Poltergeists made Henry Robinson so ill he had to be taken to hospital in order to recover from their activities in his house. Mr Robinson was eighty-six. He lived in Eland Road, Lavender Hill, Battersea, for twenty-five years without any kind of ghostly disturbance to upset him. But on November 29th, 1927, a poltergeist began haunting Mr Robinson and his family.

Six people lived in the house in Eland Road. Mr Robinson, his son Fred who was then twenty-seven, three daughters, and the son of one of the daughters, Peter.

Fred Robinson told the story:

On November 29th lumps of coal and pieces of soda and pennies began to fall on the conservatory – a lean-to building at the back of the house. It stopped for a few days. It began again in December. It struck me as being extremely curious at the time that although the pieces of coal were very small they broke the glass.

Things became so serious that I decided to call the police. I had no other idea except that some person was throwing things over the garden wall.

A constable came along, and together we stood

in the back garden and kept watch. Pieces of coal and pennies crashed on to the conservatory roof, but we could not trace their flight. One lump of coal hit the constable's helmet. He ran to the garden wall, but there was nobody there.

On December 19th our washerwoman said she would not work any longer in the house. She came to me in a state of terror and pointed to a heap of red-hot cinders in the outhouse. There was no fire near. How could they have got there?

Again I called the constable, and we decided to watch in the kitchen. Two potatoes were hurled in while we were sitting there.

It was on Monday that the climax came – at nine o'clock in the morning – and for an hour the family was terror-stricken. My sister ran to tell the magistrate. The window panel in my father's bedroom was smashed, and as he was in such a state of shock I decided to remove him from the house. I called the man from across the street, and together we carried him from the room. Just as we were taking him out a heavy chest of drawers crashed to the floor in the bedroom.

Previously my sister had seen the hall-stand swaying and had called me. I caught it before it fell, but some strange power seemed to tear it from my hands, and it fell against the stairs, breaking in two parts.

The police decided that Fred Robinson himself was responsible for what was going on. They must have thought he was mentally ill, for they took him away to hospital for an examination.

While Fred was away his sister, Mrs Perkins, the mother of young Peter, saw chairs 'march down the hall in single file'. Three times she tried to set the table for Saturday dinner but each time the chairs piled themselves up onto the table and prevented her from finishing her work. She reported this to the police but they refused to listen and said Mrs Perkins was moving the chairs herself.

The furniture was seen to move round the house unaided so many times that young Peter was afraid to sit down in case his chair was taken from under him. Like his grandfather, Peter had eventually to go off for a rest to friends in the country.

In the end only two of the women remained in the Eland Road house. The poltergeist must have had its fun, for then it disappeared and the Robinson family settled back into normal life.

CHAPTER TWELVE

The Grey Lady of Jarolen House

Jarolen House is set in the Rodborough area of the Cotswold town of Stroud. It is the home of Leo and Joyce Bennett and their daughter Elizabeth. Mr and Mrs Bennett do not believe in ghosts; but they have no foolproof explanation for the events that have taken place both in their house and in the house next door. The Bennetts are friends of mine, and it was while I was staying with them for a few months that I first heard about the Grey Lady.

Jarolen House was once the Rodborough church rectory. Some years ago the beautiful seventeenth-century building was sold and converted into two houses. One half, now called the Old Rectory, contains the old kitchen; the other half, Jarolen House, contains the original entrance hall and main staircase.

The Bennetts arrived about twelve years ago, not very long after the alterations had been made. In the summer of that year Mr and Mrs Bennett and Elizabeth went on holiday, leaving the house in the charge of Mrs Bennett's mother, Mrs Morrell.

Mrs Morrell had no sooner settled in when her son

Paul arrived home from the RAF, sick with a high temperature. Paul was put to bed at once in the main bedroom. From the windows you can look out across the tree-lined garden and the small park at the bottom of the drive, and over the square-towered church a few hundred yards down the hill, and then across the valley to Selsley Common that rises on the other side. It is a lovely room at any time, and a good place to be ill – if you have to be ill at all.

The doctor was called. He examined Paul, found nothing seriously wrong, left some pills, and went away.

A little while later Mrs Morrell peeped into the bedroom to see how Paul was feeling. He was awake, and he said, 'Who was the old lady who came into my room?'

Mrs Morrell was puzzled. She was alone in the house, and no one had come in since the doctor left.

'Nobody has been into your room,' she said.

'Yes,' said Paul, 'there has been. She was an old lady dressed in grey. She came earlier.'

Sensibly, Mrs Morrell dismissed Paul's story as the dreaming of a sick man. After all, he had a high temperature, and the doctor had given him some drugs. He was no doubt a little delirious and could not distinguish between his dreams and reality. Whatever it was, Mrs Morrell did not take Paul seriously. Nothing more was said about what he had seen.

'She was an old lady dressed in grey'

Some years later, Paul married. Whenever he and his wife Pat came to visit the Bennetts, Pat would refuse to go upstairs alone. She said she felt nervous on the landing (which, it is true, is dark and windowless). The Bennetts used to laugh at this. But Paul told his sister that he too felt uncomfortable on the landing and always had done. He did not like to make his wife more nervous still so he never mentioned this to her. The Bennetts said it was all nonsense, and passed off Pat's fears with a joke.

Then, one evening when Pat and Paul were visiting, the Bennetts' next-door neighbour, Mrs Rudd, came in. They all sat talking about quite ordinary things and spent the evening happily. At one point, Pat went upstairs. When she came down she said to Mrs Bennett, 'There's something different about your house. That grey lady isn't on the landing any more.'

The conversation stopped at once. Though she had talked about a strange feeling, she had never mentioned seeing anyone. Nor had Paul ever mentioned to her about the grey lady he saw while he was ill years before.

The silence was broken by Mrs Rudd.

'No,' she said, 'she isn't here any more because she has come to me.'

Naturally, everyone wanted to know what she meant.

In Mrs Rudd's part of the building the old kitchen had been converted into a dining-room, and a new kitchen, large and modern, had been built onto the back of the house. One day that week, Mrs Rudd recalled, she had been ironing in the kitchen when she felt that someone was watching her. She looked up and saw a figure standing in the passage outside the kitchen (which was part of the old house) and peering through the doorway at her.

The two women looked at each other a moment. Then the figure in the passage went away. It had all taken only a few seconds. But Mrs Rudd felt no fear or shock and only when the figure disappeared did she wonder who it was. She walked into the passage and looked around but could see no one. She knew her daughter Judy was somewhere in the house and thought it might have been her. So Mrs Rudd called out, 'Judy, where are you?'

'I'm upstairs,' replied Judy. 'I'm cleaning my room, as you told me to do.'

'Have you been down here in the last few minutes?' asked Mrs Rudd.

'No, why?' shouted Judy.

Mrs Rudd could not explain whom she had seen. But she did have a strong feeling that the person watching her was curious to see all that was going on, as though she had never seen anyone ironing before. And Mrs Rudd could recall clearly what the woman wore:

a long grey dress with a stiff, white, broad collar, and cuffs, and a white cap-like head-dress.

That, said Paul and Pat, was just like the woman they had seen!

Mrs Rudd saw the grey lady at other times after this. Always she was peering into the kitchen watching closely as Mrs Rudd went about her domestic chores. Never did Mrs Rudd feel frightened. Just the opposite, in fact. She rather liked the grey lady.

It was Mrs Bennett's niece, Ruth, who next mentioned the ghost. Ruth was three or four at the time and was staying a few days at Jarolen House. She had gone into the park to play. When she came in, she said to her aunt, 'Who was that old lady looking at me out of the sitting-room window?'

'Are you sure?' said Mrs Bennett. 'I don't think there was anyone there.'

'Oh yes,' said Ruth, 'there was someone looking at me from the window.'

'Perhaps it was grandmother,' said Mrs Bennett, and let the matter drop. Mrs Morrell was certainly in the house, but Mrs Bennett knew she could not have been in the sitting-room just at that moment.

No more has been seen of the grey lady since then. Not that Mrs Bennett believes it really was a ghost that Pat or Paul or Mrs Rudd or Ruth saw. She does not believe it even after what happened to her in the attic!

At the top of a steep, narrow stairway that leads off

the main landing where Pat and Paul used to feel a presence, are two attic rooms. One is a study which Mr Bennett uses when he wants to work quietly away from the family. The second room is long, with a little window at one end which is jammed permanently shut. In this room, on wet days, Mrs Bennett hangs the laundry until she is ready to iron. She has, she says, never much cared for the place: it is a little dark and somehow unpleasant.

One day she went to the attic to get some things that were hanging there. As she walked into the room a cold chill ran down her spine and the hairs on the back of her head stood up. She felt very uneasy, but was determined to get what she had come for.

She went to the centre of the room where an unshaded light hangs down from the ceiling. To switch on the light you have to reach up and press a button in the socket that holds the bulb. Mrs Bennett reached up to the socket, but before she could press the button, the light came on of its own accord.

She now felt more than ever uncomfortable, if not a little afraid. But she reminded herself that she did not believe in the supernatural; and anyway, she was certainly not going to be frightened out of her own attic! It was perfectly simple, she thought: the bulb was loose in its socket and had somehow made contact as she reached up to it.

To show herself that she was not afraid and to keep

up her courage, she decided to sing a song. All that she could think of on the spur of the moment was *Rudolph the Red-nosed Reindeer* – a song she hated! Nothing daunted, she began to sing. Anyone who has heard Mrs Bennett singing knows what a curious noise filled Jarolen House attic that day! It maybe even startled the ghost, if ghost there were. For the first verse was not finished before two sheets that were hanging on the line billowed out suddenly, just as though someone had walked into them. Then they fell back, and hung limp and still again. The other things on the line did not move at all.

Startled, Mrs Bennett stopped singing and stared at the washing on the line. Not a movement. Then, as suddenly as it had come, the uneasy feeling left her. 'Ah well,' she thought, 'it was just one of those things.' She began taking down the laundry.

But she did not get far. Downstairs, Bunty, the family's pet dog, began to bark frantically; in the way she did if anyone came to the house whom she did not much like. Mrs Bennett thought someone had arrived, and she had not heard the knock. She left the attic and went downstairs.

She found the front door closed, and no one inside or out. But Bunty was lying in her basket under the stairs, shivering and whimpering with fright.

These are the facts of what happened. Joyce Bennett leaves speculation about them to others. Was the chill that ran up her spine, and her hair standing on end caused by the state of her health that day? Or by draughts blowing through the attic? And the billowing sheets. Was that caused by a freak wind that found its way for a second through some crack in the roof of the old house? And Bunty's terrified fit. Had someone come to the door and been frightened off by the dog's barking? Or was there a ghost? And did it leave the attic (scared off by Mrs Bennett's singing!) and go downstairs, giving Bunty a fright?

There just might be an explanation. When the Bennetts moved in to Jarolen House the bells that were used to summon the servants in the old days were still there. They were fixed so that they rang in two places: in the old kitchen, and in the upstairs attic where Mrs Bennett hangs the laundry. It is more than likely that the attic was used by the 'between maid' as her bedroom.

The between maid was so called because she was shared between the housekeeper and the cook. It was her duty to do the chores: carrying coal and tending fires, answering bells, washing up. And ironing. And seeing to the needs of the children in the house. And even to answering calls at night, should anyone want things done then, which was why the bells rang in her bedroom. It was a hard life.

The Rodborough rectory was lived in for over sixty years by the Reverend Thomas Glascott. He died aged eighty-four in 1876, the father of many children. The house had eight inside servants and two outside. And as the between maid often had to fetch and carry as much for the other servants as she did for the family, she had plenty to do – and all for perhaps six or eight pounds a year in pay.

It would be nothing to wonder at if the spirit of the between maid still lingered in the Jarolen House attic, and wandered the house to see a modern house-wife doing all the chores she herself had once done, but doing them now so much more easily and cleanly and quickly. That would certainly explain the grey lady's interest in Mrs Rudd's ironing. For to a 'tween maid, a modern electric steam iron, not to mention all the other labour-saving gadgets, would seem like a magic thing, and fascinating too.

Whatever the truth is, I like to think the grey lady of Jarolen House is the between maid still shuffling round the house, keeping an eye on all the small details of family life. And certainly whenever I visit the Bennetts I keep a hopeful watch out for the old woman in a grey dress and a white starched collar and cuffs. She is a ghost I would be happy to meet.

If you have enjoyed this
PICCOLO Book, you may like
to choose your next book
from the new PICCOLO titles
listed on the following pages.

True Adventures and Picture Histories

TRUE ADVENTURES
A magnificent new series for boys and girls

Piccolo Fiction

Puzzles and Games